# ONE NIGHT

J. AKRIDGE

Cover Design: Amanda Walker PA & Design Services

Editing: Literary Edits

Formatting: J. Akridge

*For everyone who has joined me on this journey.*

# ABOUT THE AUTHOR

J. Akridge is a contemporary romance author that has a quirky sense of humor and enjoys sweet, sexy, feel good romance. She likes her bun messy, her sweats comfy, and her coffee strong. She resides in Missouri with her husband and their three children, a Great Danes named Molly, and tiny Yorkie named Jack. She's experiencing her own happily ever after with her high school sweetheart.

Since publishing her first book in 2020, she's been inspired to continue writing the love stories that play out in her head each day .

She loves to hear from her readers so make sure you check her out on social media or sign up for her newsletter to stay up to date on all her latest releases and sales.

# One
# NIGHT

## J. AKRIDGE

# 1

## TESSA

I'VE BEEN busy unpacking my new apartment all day. I'm exhausted, cranky, and sick of breaking boxes down after I've emptied them. My new apartment is small, but it's just what I need - two decent size bedrooms and a kitchen that opens to the main living area offering a spacious layout.

It's nice to finally be on my own, no rules but my own.

I deserve a break. So, I'm taking one. And what better way to take a break in, than a drink at one of the local bars?

The bar isn't far from my apartment, which is one of the things that drew me in about my location. It's easy access to restaurants, shopping, literally everything. I step up to the first bar I come to.

*Arrow.*

It's located on the corner of the street, the door at the perfect angle for easy access on both sides. I watch as people walk in from both, never missing a beat in their conversations. The building looks worn on the outside, but as soon as I cross the threshold inside, the look changes.

It has a warm glow from the twinkling lights hanging from the beams of the exposed ceiling. Large pieces of tin metal are hung along the walls giving it a rustic tone. The wooden bar top stretches from one end to the other, with large leather wrapped stools that are evenly placed along it. Several high tables are scattered around in different areas with an entire row of booths along the back. It has at least four large televisions with different sporting events on each.

The music is loud, but not so loud that you're unable to think straight. I step up to the bar and take an open seat near the end. I glance at the bartenders. One is short, possibly standing about 5'6", with sandy blonde hair that is styled perfectly without a strand out of place. He makes quick work of filling a few drink orders for some girls, while he openly flirts with each. Both giggling at whatever he's just said to them. I watch for a moment, enamored by how easy going he seems to be, completely in his element.

My eyes move to the other man, he's much taller. At least, a foot difference. His hair is black, but messy on top. He has the hair that works; the type that is messy, but looks exactly how it should. And the beard he's sporting is a freaking turn on. It's black like his hair, and he obviously takes the time to groom it. From where I'm sitting, I have a decent view of him. He has deep blue eyes that stand out against his dark hair and a defined jawline. His lips are full and it's obvious he doesn't miss any sessions at the gym. The black shirt he's wearing hugs his chest like glue and damn, if it doesn't make my mouth water. I'm not usually into guys with tattoos, but I'm digging them on him.

I grab the menu that is laying in a stack on the bar in front of me. I slowly flip through to see what all is offered.

I'm actually surprised to see so many different types of meals. Most of the bars I go to only have the typical bar food; chips and dip, wings, those types of things.

"What can I get ya?" a deep voice asks. I look up and realize it's the dark-haired bartender. His eyes shine even bluer now that he's standing in front of me, and his lips are tilted in the sexiest smirk. He knows exactly how to work his audience.

Closing the menu, I lay it back on the bar in front of me and place both my hands-on top. I lean onto my elbows slightly to get closer to the bartender. His eyes flick down to my breasts before his smirk grows, and his eyes bounce back to mine. Uh huh, he's obviously impressed by my boobs. Thankfully, I have a good set. It gives me new confidence.

"What's the best around here?" I ask. My voice is low and I'm sure he gets the memo.

I'm not normally this forward, but being in a new city, where no one knows who I am or what my past is, gives me a sense of freedom. A year ago, this Tessa wouldn't even be thought of, hell even three days ago, I wouldn't have been this forward.

"Well, we have the best beer on tap." He pauses before looking at his co-worker. "Tony over there, he is a beast at mixing drinks." He hooks his thumb towards Tony, he looks our way with a wink before he turns back to mixing drinks. A cocky smile on his perfectly polished face.

"Then I guess, give me your best beer." He grins before pushing off the bar and grabs a tall glass stacked underneath. He moves towards the dispensers and quickly pours my drink, before sliding it in front of me, quickly filling one of his own.

"Cheers," he says, before clinking my glass on his own. I watch as his glass rises to his lips and he takes a large drink, his Adam's apple bobbing as he swallows. Peeling my eyes away is damn near painful.

I lift the glass to my lips, taking a drink. The dry liquid slides down my throat, leaving a warm finish as I take the time to look around the bar. It seems to be a place all the locals love to occupy. Several groups are positioned throughout the open floor, there is a small dance floor that has maybe ten to fifteen people on it currently. Everyone is gathered around, talking to one another as if they've known each other their entire lives.

The song changes and it's one of my favorites. It was just released, but it has the best tempo. One thing I do know I have going for me is my body. I'm not overly tall, but I stand at 5'6 and I have a small waist. But, that's not all. I have a good set of boobs and an ass that I know I'm good at shaking. Not in a hooker way. Scratch that.

I down what is left of my beer and set the glass down on the bar top. I cringe as the liquid moves down my throat, the beer is no longer cold. Swinging my legs to the side of the bar stool, I make my way to the dance floor, which is filling up with more dancing drunks. I'm glad I'm letting loose a little, I feel like my entire life has been on the fast track since I lost my mom and then eventually lost my dad, too. Bouncing from foster home to foster home wasn't fun, but it did teach me that if I wanted anything good in life, I'd have to work my ass off to get it. And here I am. Working it.

My hips begin moving to the beat of the song once my feet hit the makeshift dance floor. A group of girls moves to the side slightly allowing me to join in dancing with them. We all dance for a few more songs before I feel a pair of hands on my hips.

As I turn to see who it is, I'm shocked when those dark blue eyes from the bar meet mine. I'm no expert at attending bars, but I don't think it's typical for bartenders to skip work and join the dance party. But I'm sure as hell not complaining.

"You again." I smile as I start to move my body against his to the song.

"Me again," he whispers in my ear. Chills rise on my arms and the hairs stand to attention. "You having a good time tonight?" His voice is deep against my ear and the sound goes straight to my panties. I smile back at him and answer his question by pressing my back side into his front. A low groan slips past his lips and I smile in reply.

I glance back at him and go weak in the knees. His eyes are my weakness, especially against that dark hair of his.

"What's your name, baby?" I shake my head at his question. There's really no need to exchange pleasantries. At least, I don't think there is. Chances are I'll never see him again and I'll lose my nerve if we exchange names. He laughs at my response. "Ah. It's going to be like that, huh?" I nod again which causes him to laugh more. He has a great laugh, it's deep and one that makes you smile without even realizing it.

He turns me in his arms so that I'm now grinding against his front, one of his legs is thrust between mine. The song ends, but we continue dancing through the next few. He wraps my arms around his neck, and I use the opportunity to run my hands through his hair. His hair is so freaking soft, that I can't seem to pull my hands away from it and accidently give it a slight tug.

"God, that felt so good," he groans, pulling his bottom lip between his teeth. My eyes are glued to his mouth now.

*I love the way his arms feel wrapped around me.*

I move my hands down to his neck as we continue dancing. After a few moments, he whispers in my ear again.

"Move your hands back to my hair, it felt so good," he says, breathlessly. And I do as I'm asked because, let's be honest, I nearly refused to remove my hands in the first place. I wonder what he uses to make his hair so soft?

His hand softly brushes my chin, turning it to the side so that my neck is fully exposed to him. He starts dropping little kisses to my shoulder before slowly moving up my neck. His tongue makes contact with my skin, which causes me to groan and leaves my skin feeling slightly dampened.

The touch of his lips against my skin is nearly too much, so I grip his hair and pull his mouth to mine. Our tongues touch in a frenzy, but when he gently bites down on my bottom lip, I lose all control. We are meshed together on the dance floor and probably look like we're about to be the next stars on Pornhub, but do I care? Oh, hell no, I don't because this fucking kiss is the hottest I have ever had.

No guy has ever kissed me this way before, he dominates, and it is such a turn on.

Just when I think I might actually begin dry humping this guy on the dance floor, he pulls away. I pout in the process, and he laughs before placing his lips against mine once more. He is clearly as disappointed as I am in breaking away from that kiss. I keep my eyes closed as I regain my composure and look around. Several women are staring at the two of us together, snarls fit across their faces like I've just stolen their man.

One woman stands out in particular. She has long red fingernails that stand to attention against the whiskey glass she is holding. Her lips are the same awful color. Her eyes bore into mine from across the dance floor, before they flick to the man beside me. I follow her attention and smile slightly when I realize he isn't paying her a bit of attention.

"I'm finished for the night." He glances back to the bar where Tony is working to fill orders. When he catches us looking, he gives a wink and a wave. "Do you want to have a drink or do you want to just get out of here for the night?"

Do I? Want to leave with him? Am I capable of having a night of no strings attached sex? I'm not sure, but before I can form any coherent thoughts on why this is a terrible idea, I'm nodding my head yes, and allowing him to lead me off the dance floor.

I'm sure as hell about to find out if I can do this, because if I'm this worked up over just dancing with this guy, who knows what will happen when he gets my clothes off.

# 2

# TESSA

HE GRABS my hand as we are weaving through the bodies of the bar as we make our way to the exit. I'm unsure where we are heading, and I realize this is completely reckless of me, but I don't care at the moment. My sense of self control is long gone, and my head is spinning with a mixture of the alcohol I've consumed and that kiss.

*God, that kiss. Those lips.*

The way his body presses against mine just as his lips make contact. The feel of how his hands roam my body and how his tongue gently parts my lips.

He pulls me into the cool night air, and I shiver at the contact. He notices and places an arm around my shoulders in an  attempt to provide some warmth, and it works because just the slightest touch from him has my skin burning again. He leads me to the left of the bar entrance and into a well-lit alley.

At least if he tries to attempt to kill me here, he will be seen. He pulls me up the fire escape, and  I barely make it up in these heels. Thankfully, his hands never leave my body. The door above the bar is metal and completely fits the vibe of the building. When he pushes the door open, it's dark. Only a small lamp in the corner is lit and I can vaguely make out the furniture. It's fully furnished.

"Do you live here?" I ask, as I turn towards him. His hands are already roaming over my body.

"Not anymore." Before I'm able to question him, his mouth smashes into mine and the thoughts of this apartment disappear. My hands move under his shirt slowly pulling it up before he pulls at the collar and shrugs it over his head.

*Fuck.* That body.

He is gorgeous standing before me in nothing but his ripped jeans that hang low on his hips. My eyes roam down his torso and my mouth waters. No, it actually waters at the sight of him. That's a first, although all the men I've been with before looked nothing like him. His arms are sculpted and as he balls his t-shirt in his hands before tossing it aside, I take note of how his muscles move. His abs. My god, pure perfection. My eyes glance lower until I take in the dip of his V before it disappears into his jeans.

I can already tell this will be a great night.

"I can't wait to eat every inch of you," he says, as he buries his nose into my neck, slowly nibbling at my sensitive skin. His hands move up and down my hips and thighs as he slowly pushes me backwards towards the bed.

Our lips are tangled again, and he groans into my mouth before pulling back to look down at me. Those dark blue eyes are dangerous to my self-control and he knows it. His lips are full, and I press my lips to his once more. This time, I gently bite his bottom lip, earning myself a growl.

He drops to his knees on the floor and slowly unhooks

the heels I'm wearing tonight. He slips the straps from my ankles with his fingers, which makes me weak in the knees. Once he's finished and has tossed my shoes aside, his hands slowly glide up my thighs and unbutton my denim shorts. He hooks his fingers in the belt loops and gives a quick tug, so they fall to the floor around my ankles. I step out and kick them to the side when his eyes meet mine.

I'm thinking he's going to remove my underwear next, but he shocks me when he leans in and places his tongue over my underwear directly on my center. I'm already wet from his teasing, but this is damn near too much. My hands move to his hair as my head falls back to my shoulders from the sensation.

He stands and edges me to the bed where I collapse backwards. I laugh as he crawls up my body. He straddles my waist and then moves my shirt upward exposing my lace bra I tossed on before going out tonight. And thank the good heavens I did. Typically, I dress for comfort, but most of my things are still unorganized in my apartment, regardless of how much unpacking I've done today, this set just happened to be sitting on top when I changed.

I raise my head and arms so he can easily pull it off. His fingers move to the straps of my bra as he pulls my arms free and then pulls both cups down exposing my bare flesh to him.

His mouth dips down and takes one of my nipples into his mouth. His tongue swirls, building a sensation between my legs. My hands grip the sheets underneath me as he continues his assault before switching to the other nipple. He reaches behind my back and unclasps my bra in one motion. Obviously having done this before.

He trails kisses down my stomach, his tongue leaving a

wet mark where it touches. When he reaches my under-wear, he looks up at me, silently asking if this is ok. I nod my head and move my hands to hook the edge of my underwear, and slowly begin pushing them down my thighs as far as I can, before he takes over and pulls them the rest of the way. My legs fall to the side and I'm now on full display for him.

He licks his lips and I'm now the one groaning. He leans in placing gentle kisses to the side of my thigh, before switching to the other side and repeating the motion. My body is already on fire from his soft touches and teasing.

He blows hot air onto my center and my spine tightens. He pushes my legs open wider and his tongue darts out, slowly licking.

"Oh God, don't stop," I pant, as he adds a finger to my now slick pussy.

"Fuck, you taste so good," he says, before his tongue circles my clit and he suck's it into his mouth.

He enters a second finger and curls it inwards and strokes that magic spot that causes me to become very vocal. I should be embarrassed, but it feels too good to even bother right now.

"Yes, right there." Arching my back causes him to go deeper. "Don't fucking stop." I can feel the beginning of my orgasm, and obviously he can also, because he moves his mouth back to my clit again and sucks, hard.

And then I scream, "Yes!" as I start spiraling.

# 3

# TESSA

HOLY SHIT. That orgasm. I've never had one that was so intense. I'm not sure I could stand right now if I tried.

He wipes his mouth with the back of his hand before he smirks at me. Cocky bastard knows exactly what he just did, and he did not disappoint.

He reaches to the nightstand and pulls a condom out of the drawer. He hands it to me, and I place it between my lips, but pause before ripping the package open. I undo the button of his jeans and he slips them off followed by his underwear, I glance down at his dick. The thick erection sends a shiver down my spine. He's hard, standing at full attention as I wait for him to crawl onto the bed. I push him to the side, so he falls to his back.

I slowly crawl over him and drop the packet to his chest before placing my lips against his. Once I'm satisfied and sure he's worked up, I move myself down his body. My lips grazing his skin to tease him the way he did me, over and over.

I grab his penis in my hand, and I should be terrified

that my fingers don't wrap all the way around him, but I'm more excited now than I was before. His eyes follow my every movement and I'm so turned on by it. A sudden burst of bravery pushes me forward, so I graze my hand over the tip, and he groans, throwing his head back against the pillows.

His reaction sparks a confidence in me I've never had before, so I use it to slowly press my lips to him. He groans so I reach my tongue out and circle the tip before sucking it into my mouth. My hand moves to the base and I slowly begin pumping him while I continue to swirl my tongue.

My assault doesn't last as long as I'd have liked before he pushes me off and throws me against the pillows in one movement. I giggle as he takes the condom from the bed and rips the package open with his teeth.

*My God, he's sexy.*

He rolls the condom down and settles at my entrance.

"Pull your legs around me, baby." I do as he says and he tugs me forward so the tip of his penis is now resting against my opening. It's warm and causes me to lose my train of thought.

He slowly moves his shaft up and down, making me wetter just by the small sensation. I could explode just by this simple movement.

He slowly pushes inside and I can feel every ridge of him as he slides all the way in.

"God. Yes!" he says, as he pushes deep. "You are so fucking tight." I squeeze him and tighten my legs around his waist. He drops his forehead to mine and I take a moment to adjust to his size.

He feels amazing.

I raise my hips and slowly slide back onto him. He

starts moving, his hips meeting mine, stroke for stroke. I can already feel the sensation building low in my tummy.

He teases me, slowing his tempo and then rapidly picking back up. Once I hit the point of losing control, he slows again.

Both of us are now covered in sweat, and his hand slides from my neck down between my breast. His palm is pressed flat against my stomach as he keeps moving downward. His thumb slides over my clit and he presses down.

"Come for me, baby." And I do. I come so hard I see stars. I hear nothing but white noise and his heavy breathing, as he continues to pound into me until he reaches his own climax.

"Holy fuck," he says, as his body collapses on mine and his arm moves over his face as his breathing continues at a rapid pace.

After we clean up, he pulls me into his side before we both fall asleep.

# 4

# KYLE

My eyes slowly slide open, I smile to myself when the memories of the night flood back in. Reaching over, my hand connects with nothing but the mattress underneath me. I turn my head, looking at the empty half of my bed.

She's gone.

Fuck. I *never* sleep with the same girl twice, at least not unless it was sex like last night. But I've *never* fallen asleep with one the way I did her. There's really no reason for it, I've not been scorned by a past lover or had a terrible childhood with a parent who abandoned me and left me with commitment issues, it's just how I operate.

Standing, I walk to my bathroom and flip the light on. After I take a piss, I look at myself in the mirror. My hair is disheveled from sleep, I slowly run a hand through it. The thought of how her hands felt when they were in my hair makes me hard. I shake my head and walk over to the shower, turning the nozzle until the temperature is where I want it.

The water cascades down my body, soothing my

muscles. Thoughts of her wrapped around me swirl throughout my head, the way she felt pressed against my body. My hand moves lower until I reach my dick. Wrapping my hand around it, I begin moving it. My thumbs swipes over the top, wiping away the precum. I think about how her body looked, naked against my bed. A groan erupts from my throat as I move my hand quicker, working myself towards that spiral of pleasure. My mind moves to the way she tastes, how her body jerked when I touched her sensitive spot.

The thought sends me over the edge, spiraling into bliss. My forehead falls against the shower wall, the water washing away any remains of my dirty thoughts of her. I fucking wish I knew her name, or how to find her.

Not exchanging names was one of the biggest fuck ups, because I sure as hell didn't know that last night would feel like that.

———

WHEN I WALK into the bar, all the lights are on. It's a different scene from the night version that I'm used to. Each day, I come in for a few hours in the morning to work on the books, restock anything we ran low on the night before, and get things in order for the next night.

"There you are." Tony laughs as I step behind the bar. Tony's been with me since I opened, he's a magician at mixing drinks. "I figured you'd be here sooner."

"Overslept." I lie. I don't want to tell him about everything going on in my fucking head, or how I couldn't get enough of the girl from last night that I had to give myself a hand job in the shower just to get through the day. He doesn't respond, just continues wiping down glasses and stacking them under the bar.

One we're finished, he moves to stand in front of where I'm working. "Have a nice night?" he smirks, he's constantly busting my balls after nights when I leave with a woman.

"Shut the fuck up." I laugh, I keep reviewing the books from last night. The bar keeps getting busier and I'm so proud of how far it's come. When I opened it, I didn't think it'd do a good job. But, my bar offers a vibe that you don't get in many other places in the city and I think that's why it's become so popular.

"You going to call her?" he asks. Fuck, I wish.

"Nah." It's not a lie, I don't have a way to call her. "Didn't get her name, or number. You know how I work." He does, he's been with me for years and knows I don't sleep with the same girl twice.

"Shame," he says. "She was fucking hot."

"You're not wrong." I add, he stands from his stool.

"Alright, I'm heading out. Try to sleep a little more before shift tonight." He pats his fist against the bar before turning and walking towards the exit.

"See you later." I say, he throws a hand in the air in what looks like a wave but I'm not sure.

I spend the rest of the day thinking about the girl with dark hair and perfect body. Wondering if I'll see her again.

# 5

# TESSA

IT'S BEEN NEARLY six weeks since my night with the hot bartender. After our night together, we both passed out. When I woke up, it was nearly four in the morning, so I grabbed my things that were scattered around the floor, took one last look at the naked, handsome man that lay asleep on the bed, and snuck out the door.

My first one-night stand was a success and I don't regret it. The only thing I regret is not getting his name. I've been too embarrassed to go back to the bar after I snuck out. The whole one night stand thing freaked me out and I'm not sure the correct way to handle it all. Besides, how do I even know he wanted to see me again? We were pretty clear that it was one night, which is why I was insistent on not giving him my name.

I've managed to get a job at a real-estate company here and so far, I'm loving it. My co-workers are wonderful and I'm able to do most of my work from home, which is really nice when I wake up feeling like having a lazy morning. I've even managed to make a few friends, which has been great in a city where I don't know a single soul.

Being in and out of foster care left me with no family and rarely any friends. No one wanted to get close to the poor, pitiful, foster child. Lucky for me, when I turned eighteen and aged out of the system, the foster family I had been living with allowed me to stay with them another year in order to focus on getting my real estate license. Once I did that, I stayed and got the ropes of working the business, but eventually I needed out of the town where everyone knew every little detail of my past life and judged me for things that were out of my control.

It was a logical choice for me, real estate is a good money maker when you work the market correctly and I needed the security. That's exactly what I've gotten. I don't have a fortune, but I'm taken care of. I have a nice apartment and it's furnished with food. Something that I didn't always have in foster care. Most of the homes were good and the people were nice, but I was in a few places that would make a judge cringe if he knew what really went on.

"Tacos after your last meeting?" Chloe askes. Chloe is one of my coworkers that I hit it off with instantly. Our personalities are one in the same and we are both new to the city, which is what really bonded us. She's a feisty thing, always has something to say and is quick with the comebacks. She has beautiful red hair, but not the red that makes you feel sorry for the amount of sunscreen she has to use. She is tall for a female, standing about 5'8 or so.

"You got it. I'm heading there now. Meet you in about an hour?" I say, as I head towards the exit of the building. My car sits along the edge of the street, it's small but I really didn't need anything large. It was my first purchase when I sold my first house a few years ago and it's been a great vehicle.

I climb into my car and head towards the house I'm showing. The family is eager to move and the owners are ready to sell, so hopefully this will be a quick close if they all love the offers I have to present.

When I arrived at the property, I put my car in park before climbing out. I'm a little earlier than my clients, but I like it this way. Gives me a chance to get inside before they do and do a quick walk through and remember the important selling features of the home. I show so many homes each week, that they sometimes begin to run together. The last thing I need is to suggest going to see the pool in the backyard, only to be greeted with a giant lot of green grass.

This house is a large two-story home, it has a large yard which is something the Brown's stressed was a need with their small family. They have two little girls, ages seven and three.

I hear cars opening after I've done my walk through and I head to the front door.

"Hello," I say, as I step onto the front porch to greet them all. "What do you think?" Mrs. Brown looks around, sporting a wide smile as she takes in the exterior of the home. Bright white siding frames the entire exterior, but it is accented with black shutters and a gorgeous wrap-around porch.

"It's gorgeous, Tessa." She steps forward and shakes my hand. Mr. Brown follows behind.

"The yard looks like it's a decent size." He moves to shake my hand.

"It is. I think you'll be impressed with the backyard." I

place my hand in his and give a firm squeeze. "Shall we?" I turn and lead them inside the main living space. After we have discussed the size of the home, I allow them to wander freely to check everything out. I've learned it's easier to let them search the home this way and it proves to be a smart strategy in selling for me. If they have questions, then they can come find me, otherwise they roam and fall in love at their own pace.

When they return, I have copies of everything prepared in case they are ready to make an offer on the home, as well as some copies of details about the home for them to take with them.

"It is absolutely perfect, Tessa. And it's a good thing there is a fourth bedroom." She smiles at her husband and I tilt my head to the side. "I noticed this morning that I'm a few weeks late on my period. So, we decided to take a quick test and it was positive." She nearly jumps with joy and I can't help but follow suit in her excitement. Anytime someone mentions their period, I always think about mine, which is slightly late, but nothing out of the ordinary with my lifestyle. I've never had regular periods, they are all over the place. About like the weather.

"This is the home for us. Where do we sign?" Mr. Brown says, after hugging his wife. He pulls a pen from his shirt pocket and clicks it showing how ready he is to sign.

I pull the packet out and show him where to sign on each page, his wife does the same, signing below his name.

"Congratulations, guys. I'm so happy for you. A new baby and a new home." I follow them out of the home and head to the trunk of my car. I pop the trunk and reach in to grab the "pending" sign that hangs from the bottoms of our real estate signs. They watch as I move across the yard and hang the sign on the hooks. It swings slightly before settling.

I turn and smile at them as they climb into their car.

I call Chloe to let her know that I'm on my way. When I arrive, she has already found us seats near the back of the restaurant. Her favorite section to sit in any restaurant. She's a people watcher so she enjoys being able to see everything and everyone.

"How did it go?" she asks, as I toss my purse into the seat between us.

"Another one sold." I smile as the waitress places two margaritas in front of us.

"You're a lucky bitch. You sell more homes than any of us on the team." She isn't wrong. "I ordered us both margaritas, too. I assumed we'd be celebrating tonight."

"You thought right." I wink at her and take a sip of my drink. We order our food and sit for a couple hours discussing the events of the past week. She has a sale pending on a property she has been trying to sell for a few months. She tells me about a guy she just met at the park where she runs in the mornings and they have their first date tomorrow night. I have never really been on a date, just a few here and there in high school when my foster parents would allow it.

Halfway through eating, I suddenly feel extremely nauseous. Which is extremely rare considering tacos are my favorite food. I can punish some Mexican food.

My mind starts wandering and I freeze. What if?

No, no. That isn't possible. I'd already know by now.

Wouldn't I? My period has been late before. It's just a false alarm like the other times. My job can be stressful and I do work a lot.

"Are you feeling ok? You're really pale all of a sudden." Chloe wipes her mouth and moves her plate to the side, she signals the waitress who comes over quickly. She orders me a water. Before she can return, I'm out of my seat and hurrying across the restaurant towards the bathrooms.

I rush into the first stall that is open and throw up immediately.

"Tessa?" Chloe enters behind me. "Are you ok?" She wets a paper towel and brings it over to me as I shift my weight to sit on the bathroom floor. I'm trying not to think of how disgusting this floor is, but I really don't think I can stand at the moment.

"Here." She hands me the paper towel and I wipe my mouth with it before tossing it into the toilet. "What was all that?"

What was all that? I rarely ever get sick; I couldn't tell you the last time I actually went to the doctor for something that wasn't just a checkup. I was blessed with good health and it's something I don't take for granted.

"I'm not sure. Maybe the tacos just didn't settle right." I turn my head to look at her. She's squatted behind me with an extra paper towel, holding it out to me. I take it and gently dab it against my forehead. The cool feeling making me feel better instantly.

"For a second there, I thought you were pregnant," she laughs and typically I would, too, but instead, I freeze. Holy shit.

What if I'm pregnant? I can't be. That's impossible. It's just another one of those months where the stress of life has altered my monthly cycle. Nothing alarming.

But what if I am? I move my eyes to meet Chloe's and

she pales at the realization of what just went racing through my mind.

"Oh shit," she says, and if this was any other situation I'd die laughing from the look on her face.

*Oh shit is right.*

# 6

# TESSA

I STOP at the drug store on my way home from dinner. Chloe insisted on coming with me, but I decided I needed to do this on my own, so she made me promise I'd call her as soon as I got the results.

I have no idea what my future holds at the moment, and it's all going to be determined by this a box that cost six dollars at a pharmacy.

When I get home, I take my time. I get changed in my night clothes; I figure either way this test goes I'll be ready for bed by the end.

I drink nearly two bottles of water while I'm opening the box and reading the directions. I bought two, just in case.

Step 1. Remove the plastic cap to expose the absorbent window. Check.

Step 2. Point the absorbent tip directly into the urine stream for at least seven to ten seconds to ensure an adequate sample is collected. Check.

Step 3. Re-cap the device and place it horizontally on a clean, flat surface. Check.

Step 4. Wait five minutes for the test to finish processing.

I pace the floor back and forth. What the hell am I going to do if I'm pregnant? I had a one night stand the night I moved to this city and I don't even know his name. Which I guess if I am pregnant, I can go back to the bar and tell him there. I bet he'll be really excited to see me. I roll my eyes and peek back over at the test. It hasn't been five minutes yet, but I'm freaking the fuck out.

I grab my phone to text Chloe. At least, she can keep me sane. Or as sane as anyone can truly keep me.

> Hey, you up?

> Yeah, how's it going?

> Waiting on the results now. The directions say it takes up to five minutes.

> Need me to come over?

> No, I think I'll be ok. I'm just going to go to bed either way. Figure it all out in the morning.

> It's probably just a false alarm and you just got worked up for nothing.

> We shall see. Times up.

> Text me.

I toss my phone on the bed and walk to my bathroom. The test sits on the edge of my bathroom vanity and even from a distance, I can see the two lines. They are dark and very clear.

*I'm pregnant.*

———

I wake up the next morning with a horrible headache. Probably from the amount of crying I did last night before my body finally shut down on me. I'm still trying to wrap my mind around the idea of me being pregnant.

When I step into my bathroom, the pregnancy test is still sitting on my vanity. The words pregnant are in bold letters. I risk a look in the mirror. My eyes are puffy and red and I look like pure hell. Feel it, too. It's been so long since I've cried myself to sleep like that.

There's a very large chance that I'll be raising this baby on my own, and that's terrifying. But I know this is the choice I need to make. Abortion isn't an option for me, and I can't imagine carrying this baby and giving it up for adoption when I'm fully capable of providing a loving home.

Having a baby at twenty-one wasn't what I planned, but it's what I've been dealt now and I'm going to make the best of it.

I walk the short distance from my car to the entrance of Arrow. It's deserted at this time of day, but I have to find the guy to let him know the news. If he doesn't want to be involved then so be it, I'll do it on my own, but he at least deserves a chance to know.

When I step inside, I'm taken aback by the bright lights. Not the twinkling little Christmas lights that hang from the ceilings like the last time I was here. These are bright and nearly hurt my eyes. I'm sure they're showing every horrible detail of my night on my face.

"We don't open until eight tonight," the man behind the bar states.

"Yes, I'm looking for someone. Maybe you can help," I say, as I step near the bar.

"What's the name?" he asks, placing a box down on the bar.

"Well, I'm not really sure. He has dark hair and blue eyes. Probably stands about 6'2" or so. He's a bartender here."

"Hmm. I don't know, sweetheart. That doesn't sound like anyone that works here, I'm new and they just fired a guy, so maybe that's who you're thinking of."

Just my luck, the dude would get fired and then I'd have no way to contact him.

"Do you know his name by chance?"

"Nah, no help. Sorry, ma'am," he says, before returning to his work.

"Is the manager here by chance? Maybe he would know who it was?" I ask. Surely, someone here can point me in the right direction.

"No, he isn't in right now. Sorry, miss."

I thank him and then head out the door. Just as I'm approaching, I remember the other bartender. I turn on my heels and approach the man again.

"I'm sorry, what about a Tony?" I ask, hoping someone can help point me in the right direction. The man stares into my eyes before nodding and heading through a doorway at the end of the bar.

My hand instinctively moves to my stomach. My flat stomach and it isn't lost on me how I feel completely different today than I did yesterday. My entire body is programmed to know that I have a child growing inside me. After a few moments, Tony steps through. He scans the bar before he finds me standing near the side closest to the exit.

"Hi, what can I do for you?" he asks, as he tosses a rag over his shoulder and crosses his arms.

"You were here the night I was here. I went home with the other bartender that was working that night."

"I'm sorry, honey. I work with a lot of bartenders that take a lot of girls home. You got a name?" he asks.

I shake my head, feeling embarrassed. When I decided not to exchange names that night, I didn't think I'd be back here a month a half later looking for him.

"He has dark hair and blue eyes."

He laughs. "Listen, if he didn't give you a name, then he isn't interested in a call back. I've known him for years and I have never known of him spending more than one night with a girl." He places his hand on my shoulder, squeezing slightly. "Take my advice and move on. Don't be one of the girls that get hung up on someone that isn't interested in what you're offering." He eyes me up and down, I'm embarrassed and feel cheap.

I stand in front of him, completely dumbfounded as I watch him walk back through the doorway to the back of the bar. Tears are starting to burn the rim of my eyes as I fight them back, I glance around the bar again before turning for the exit.

I call Chloe and tell her to meet me at her house. I've got to figure out a plan and I really just need a friend right now. I have no idea how to contact the guy and I need to figure out which doctor I'll be using.

# 7

## TESSA

### FIRST APPOINTMENT

THE WAITING room is clean and modern. It eases my nerves the moment I sit down in one of the oversized plush chairs that are lined along the walls of the waiting room. Dr. Tucker is easily the most highly spoken of obstetrician in the city and she is normally extremely difficult to get into, but Chloe knew someone that was able to call in a favor to get me in sooner.

I finish filling out the initial paperwork. All asking questions about my history and the baby's father. I hate that I'm bringing a child into this world without a father, but at least I can say I tried to find him.

Truly, my child was better off than being with a man who brings a different girl home each night and can't seem to settle down. It is rare that those men ever change.

The room is filled with pregnant women, each looking at baby magazines with their spouse, smiling happily. My heart aches at the thought of doing this by myself. I slide my hand over my flat stomach and rest it there.

"Tessa." I look up when I hear my name being called. A

short nurse stands holding the door open with a folder in her hand. I stand, collecting my bag and following her through the door. "Right this way." She holds her hand out and gestures for me to enter a room where a scale is set up. I place my bag on the chair and step up. I watch as she maneuvers the scale to get my exact weight. "One hundred and twenty-two pounds." She writes the weight in my file, before grabbing the blood pressure cuff and placing it on my arm.

The moment is silent as I watch her check my blood pressure. Once she is finished, we exit the room and enter an exam room.

"The doctor will be with you shortly." She smiles as she exits the room, but I don't miss the sad look she gives me before the door clicks shut. I know it's something I'll have to get used to. The single mother who doesn't know who the father of her baby is, how the child will be forced to live a life with no father.

I reach for my cell phone out of my bag and send a text to Chloe.

> Hey you.

> What up? What up?

> At the doctor. Waiting for her to come in now.

> How ya doing?

> Well, I haven't freaked out yet, so I suppose I'm doing halfway decent.

How's the doctor's office? They say she is one of the absolute best.

I'm excited to meet her. I've heard great things; the office is super nice. That's a plus.

That's good.

"Tessa." The door opens slowly after a soft knock to the outside. "I'm Dr. Tucker." She places my folder down beside the sink and walks the short distance to shake my hand.

"Nice to meet you," I say.

"So, today will be super short and simple." She slides a rolling stool out and takes a seat, flicking open her laptop and typing away. "It's basically just a meet and greet. We will get some blood work and schedule you for your first ultrasound."

First ultrasound? Already?

"My first ultrasound?" I ask, startled that it would happen this early. I always assumed ultrasounds were to the point when you knew the baby's sex.

"Yes, I like to keep track of the pregnancy by measuring the sack." She stops typing and turns towards me. "I'm sorry, I don't mean to be extremely forward, and truthfully it isn't any of my business, but I noticed your paperwork doesn't have a father listed or a next of kin."

I sigh. I knew this would come up eventually.

"Yes. It's a long story, but it is just me," I say, dragging my eyes to my stomach. "Well, the two of us now." I smile.

"No worries, I just wanted to be able to point you in

the right direction to get any and all the support you need during this journey."

"I appreciate that." I smile back at her, and for the first time, I feel confident that I can do this. More than I have this far.

# 8

# TESSA

I'M HEADING to meet Chloe at her apartment. It's been exactly a month since my first doctor's appointment and today I went for my first ultrasound. Chloe wanted to go, but had a showing at the same time. She offered to cancel it but I wouldn't let her.

When I pull in front of her building, I park in her designated guest space and climb out. The pictures in hand as I trot to her front door. The door opens before I even have a chance to raise my hand and knock.

"Show me." she squeals. I hold the ultrasound images up, a long line of several dropping to hang. "Oh, how cute."

"You can't even see anything." I laugh, all that's on the picture is a small little smudge that is the baby on a black and white image.

"Sure you can." she says. "There's the baby." Her eyes move to mine. "You're having a baby." I nod. "Wow."

"I know, I'm getting more excited. I'm just terrified to

do this on my own, but I know I'll be able to make it work." I sigh.

"Umm, yeah you will. You're a badass bitch." She steps away from her door and lets me walk in. "So, have you tried finding him?"

"Not since that day. I don't know where he's working now, and I don't even know a name to track him down." I sit on her couch, crossing my arms over my chest. Her TV is on and she's been watching an episode of *House Hunters*.

"Okay, so what's the plan? I'm here to help." I smile at her, she's seriously one of the best friends a girl could ever ask for.

"Well, I have a long list of things the baby will need. I guess we can start working on the nursery soon, getting it cleaned out and I need to figure out what I'm going to do about a crib and stuff." I explain.

"Oh, let me know you. I've been looking at baby bedding, and that shit is so adorable." She reaches for her phone, pulling up a website that only sells baby bedding. She scrolls through several, some are boys while some are for girls. "They're adorable."

"They really are. I like this one." I tell her, pointing at the screen. It's a pale yellow, with small little touches that make it seem so calm and quaint.

"I never would have thought you'd like that one, but it's adorable." She smiles. We spend the rest of the day discussing the baby's room and what my plans are for it. It's one of the first times I've felt prepared to have a baby on my own, and after today, I know that I'm not on my own. Because I have Chloe.

Once I left her house, I grabbed take out from my favorite restaurant on the way home. When I walk inside, I sit the food down and start rummaging through my cabinets for a plate.

Opening the lid of the takeout container, I nearly gag at the smell. I close it quickly, but the nausea doesn't ease up. Running to the bathroom, I barely make it before everything comes up.

"Ugh." I moan, falling to the floor, feeling exhausted. Morning sickness has come and gone, but it seems like it's becoming more common lately.

Dr. Tucker said it usually eases up around the second trimester, so I'm just trying to count down the days until I'm there. Praying that I get some relief from this.

I don't know how women do this over, and over. I haven't even gotten to the hardest part of the pregnancy yet and I feel like I might not make it. Standing, I grab my tooth brush and brush my teeth to get the taste out.

When my stomach growls, I head back into the kitchen to finish my food. That's the strange thing about pregnancy, you crave things that you know aren't going to settle well.

Shaking my head, I fix my plate and head to the couch to watch a new show I've been binging. Looking around, my apartment is quiet and empty, but I know that soon enough it'll have some life to it.

# 9

# TESSA

## 26 WEEKS

"HELLO. It's been a while since I have seen you." Dr. Tucker barrels through the door of the exam room, she's tall and slender with long blonde hair swept back in a ponytail that curls at the end. My last three appointments she was in delivery, so I opted to see the nurse practitioner, so I didn't have to wait as long. "How has everything been going?" She glances down at the file in her hand as she sits on the small stool across from the exam table. "I see we are having some blood pressure issues?" I nod when she looks up. "We will start seeing you every week from this point on, just to be on the safe side. Some discomfort is going to be normal. The baby will start to position itself for the birth canal soon." Flipping through a few more pages, she stops. "Tessa, have you not found out the sex of the baby yet?"

I groan. "No, every time we have attempted it, the baby made it completely impossible to see the gender." Leave it to me to end up knocked up by a stranger and also have a child that is completely stubborn.

I've come to terms with being a single parent. I'm actually quite excited to have this baby, knowing I have carried him/her inside me is a somewhat magical feeling. A little girl wouldn't be so bad, someone to dress in fancy little dresses and big bows. I'd honestly never saw myself having children, but at this point I'm so thankful I am now.

"Here. Drink this." She hands me a rather large bottle of water to drink. "I'm gonna see if we can't figure out the gender of this stubborn baby today."

I all but chug the water. And, yes. I did spill half of it down my top. Ya know, because what else could really go wrong at this point?

I lay on my back with my shirt pulled up over my round stomach with paper tucked around the waistband of my sweatpants. I turn my head, so I have a better view of the tiny screen that holds my child's picture.

"This may be cold-" She squirts the cold as hell liquid onto my stomach. Why do they always say this may be cold? You know it's going to be cold, it always it. I swear, they sit these bottles in freezers overnight just to get a good laugh out of woman who squirm when they squirt it on our stomachs. Whew, hormones.

She flicks the wand around my belly to smooth out the gel and hits a button on the keyboard. The screen lights up and you can see a gray and black picture. As she moves the wand, the image changes.

"Bum Bum, Bum Bum." The baby's heartbeat echoes through the tiny room and a tear slips from the corner of my eye. My baby. Every time I get to see my baby on the screen I have the same overwhelming feeling. I will never forget the first time I felt a kick. It was like butterflies in my stomach, but I knew without a doubt exactly what it was.

"Here." She freezes the screen and hits a few buttons before turning the screen towards me. "It almost sounds like there are two little heart beats in there but I'm only seeing one baby." Whew, thank goodness. I'm not sure I could handle more than one baby as a single mom. I turn my attention to the screen. I see ten little fingers and ten little toes, a cute button nose. She points to one section and immediately, I know the sex of my baby. There's no mistaking it.

A boy. I'm not at all mentally prepared for a boy.

————

AFTER MY DOCTOR'S APPOINTMENT, I meet Chloe at a little Mexican restaurant down the street. I'm starving and honestly, I can always eat. This baby is always hungry, and up until a few weeks ago, everything I ate caused non stop morning sickness.

I need to get a few new maternity outfits. My clothes are starting to get too tight and uncomfortable.

"Hi, momma," Chloe says, with so much enthusiasm I can't help but laugh as I step through the door of the restaurant. Heads turn at her outburst, but I keep walking to my seat trying not to make eye contact with too many on my way.

"I can't stand you." Laughing again as I set my bag down next to the table and hug her. I'm mostly working from home now and rarely stopping in the office unless it's to pick up paperwork.

"You know you love me," she says and she is right; I do.

It's hard not to. When I moved to the city, I didn't think I'd make any friends, especially not any that would stay with me. But here's Chloe, my closest friend and she didn't even bat an eyelash when I found out I was pregnant unexpectedly. She didn't judge me when I told her I had no idea who the father was, well I knew, but I couldn't track him down. She just offered comfort and support and that was exactly what I needed in this lonely world. She is the only person in my corner.

"How was your doctor's appointment?" she asks, as she opens her menu and starts searching for what she wants. She does this every time we get together for lunch, even though she eats the exact same thing from every restaurant. She will never try anything new and says it's because she is too picky, and doesn't want to waste the money if she doesn't like it. Seems reasonable enough.

"It went good. I had an ultrasound." I'm stuffing a chip in my mouth as I'm talking, and Chloe just looks at me like I'm the most disgusting person on the planet. She hates my eating habits and it's only gotten worse since I've become pregnant. I laugh at the face she is making then proceed to dramatically lick the extra salsa dip off my fingers.

"You are the most disgusting human being I have ever met." She rolls her eyes before grabbing a chip of her own where she breaks pieces off before dipping. She glances at my swollen belly. "And I hope like hell that perfect baby boy doesn't learn your manners, but takes after Aunt CoCo instead." She winks as she dips her chip in the salsa and pops it in her mouth. "How was the ultrasound? Everything still good?"

"Yeah, she scared me once because she said it sounded like there were two heartbeats, but she assured me she could only see one baby." I laugh at the thought of me being a single mom to twins. "That would have been a disaster."

"My god. Could you imagine?"

"Not at all," I say. I'm excited for this baby, it overwhelmed me at first, but I've come to terms with the idea of being a single mom. I'm ok with that, but the idea of being a single mom to not one, but two infants would have me terrified. Twice the diapers to change, twice the bottles to wash and twice the amount of sleep I wouldn't get at night. "But, I found out it's a boy," I say, giddy when I speak.

"A boy?" she shouts. I look around the restaurant, embarrassed by her outburst and start laughing at the reactions from others. I nod and she claps her hands in excitement. "That is so freaking exciting." She leans forward on her elbow and reaches for my hand, squeezing it slightly. "I'll be the best fucking aunt that boy has."

The waiter arrives to take our order and I watch as Chloe openly flirts with him, which puts him behind on placing our order. This happens every time we come; I should really learn by now.

After our food arrives, we eat in peace aside from Chloe making the occasional joke about the way I eat. I play it off because I'm pregnant and no one judges me on my eating habits while I'm pregnant. Except Chloe. When our check comes, I try to be quick and snatch it off the table, but she beats me to it and quickly jumps out of her chair with her purse to go pay. She has refused to let me pay for lunch since she found out I was pregnant, and while I'm still capable of paying and taking care of our bill, she still refuses.

"You ready?" she asks, as she returns to the table. I take another quick drink before grabbing my purse and following her towards the door. "Bye, Alejandro," she says, as she winks at our waiter. He always winks in return and the flirting continues until the next trip.

The sun outside is warm, my skin warms instantly from the cool atmosphere of the restaurant. It takes me a moment for my eyes to adjust to the brightness. It's been extremely hot lately, so I've been making sure  my outings are as short as possible when out in the heat.

"So, what kind of clothes are we needing?" She loops her arm through mine and playfully rubs my belly with her other hand.

"Something that doesn't cut me in half and will actually go up my thighs, willingly." I cut a look at her. There is a cute maternity boutique down the street, so we decide to walk. We know my round ass could use a little exercise. The boutique is shared with a boutique of stylish clothes for women who aren't pregnant, and the maternity section of the store was just added a few months ago, so I'm excited to check it out. It's so hard to find decent professional looking clothing for pregnant women.

"Hello, ladies. Can I help you find anything?" the saleswoman asks, as we step through the door. I politely tell her we are just looking, but we will let her know if we need anything.

I browse several sections and when I meet up with Chloe, I'm pleased with the selection we have. I opt to try them on considering I'm a giant whale and I don't know what size really fits me anymore. The first outfit I try on is a super cute, blue maxi dress that flows at the bottom. I step out of the dressing room to show Chloe, but I'm greeted with Vivian, the receptionist at my OBGYN. I cannot stand this girl. I know that's mean of me, considering I've only been around her a few times and only ever in the doctor's office, but she constantly makes little comments about not knowing who the father is or something about what I'm wearing. She's rude, hateful, and such a bitch. Therefore, I don't fucking like her. Pregnancy has made me bitchy. I'll admit that.

"Well, hi there, Tessa." She says my name with such disgust, that I literally have to fight the urge to throat punch her. I'd rather not get arrested for physical assault while pregnant.

"Hi, Vivian," I say, before I turn to find Chloe, trying to keep the greeting short so I can get the hell away from her.

"Funny seeing you here," she says, as I head towards where Chloe is standing.

"Yeah? Why's that?" It's the maternity side of the store. I'm pregnant. I think it makes perfect sense, but she seems a little special, so I'll humor her.

"Oh, I don't know. Just didn't' think you'd shop at a cute shop like this." I roll my eyes. Turning my back to her, I search Chloe out again.

"Chloe." When I call her name, she turns her attention from the rack she was searching toward me, her eyes travel down the blue dress and she breaks into a full-blown smile. I hold my arms out and do a slow turn for her.

"I fucking love it," she says, holding her hand up motioning for me to twirl again.

"That color does nothing for you, though." Vivian's voice is nasally behind me and I involuntarily roll my eyes at the sound. Chloe makes eye contact with me and I can tell she's about to rip her a new one. Now I just have to decide if I'll let Chloe do it or not. I'm usually the calmer friend of the duo, but sometimes you need a Chloe outburst. And by sometimes, I mean, I think now is appropriate.

"I think blue is the perfect color for her," Chloe says, as she steps closer to me, throwing an arm around my shoulder. She stares Vivian up and down and Vivian shifts her weight nervously. The movement causes me to smile slightly. "However, brown isn't your color." Chloe steps closer to her, her arm dropping from my shoulder. I can see Chloe's eyes go from head to toe as she looks at her with such disgust and hatred. "Actually, maybe it is. The color of shit looks good on you, *Viv*ian." She winks before pulling me behind her towards the dressing room. I glance back at Vivian and she stomps her feet before storming off to the exit, dragging the friend she came with behind her. I hadn't noticed the friend before now, bless her heart if she's stuck with that bitch.

"She's such a bitch." Chloe states, as she steps into the dressing room with me. I agree with a head nod. She helps pull the sleeves down over my arms and gets the rest of my clothes that I'm planning to purchase and takes them to the check out for me. When I finally get dressed and my pants are situated to where my suffocation level is minimal, I follow behind to pay for the clothes.

"I can't believe she fucking told you that you didn't look good. That whore." Chloe is still worked up over the ordeal. "I couldn't stand that bitch the first time I met her." I'm not sure what made her hate me so bad, but obviously I did something at some point. But I've never even seen the girl before my first OBGYN appointment.

"She hates me, and I still haven't figured out why," I say, as I pop the trunk on my car and place the shopping bags inside.

"She's jealous," Chloe say matter of fact. After slamming the trunk, I turn to face her. I cross my arms over my chest and let them rest on my baby bump.

"Jealous of what? My ass or this ginormous belly sticking out?" I laugh, as I say it and grab my belly for dramatics.

"You're gorgeous and you fucking know it." She winks. "You have one of the best personalities and you care. That's rare." She giggles. "And obviously, *Vivian-*"she says with an eye roll, and jerks her thumb over her shoulder, "didn't get those traits. All she got was a dry personality and a nose too small for her face."

# 10

## TESSA

### 32 WEEKS

"Your blood pressure is looking much better; have you still been taking it easy at home?" the nurse asks, as I climb onto the exam table and attempt to sit. I say attempt because me trying to climb up this table is more like watching someone attempt to climb a mountain; there are several mishaps before I'm safely in the seated position.

"Yes, I've really been working on not getting stressed so easily," I say, which is so much easier said than done. I naturally stress over the smallest things.

"Great, Dr. Tucker will be in shortly." The nurse steps into the hallway and closes the door behind her. It's time for another checkup and I'm thankful that this appointment will be short today. I'm exhausted and just ready to kick my feet up and call it a day.

A light knock at the door before it opens startles me.

"Hello, Tessa. How are we doing?" Dr. Tucker enters the room and immediately starts washing her hands, something she always does.

She moves to sit on the round stool in front of me, flipping through my chart. "Now, I want to talk about who will be present in the delivery room when the time comes." She flips through a few more pages and starts jotting things down. "Father?" She glances up and I shake my head. "Okay, either of your parents?" I shake my head again. She closes the folder and crosses her arms over it. "Tessa, do you have anyone here? To help you?" I drop my head now, embarrassed. I have no family, no friends.

I moved to this city nearly a year ago. I needed a change of scenery and thought picking up and moving off would be the best way to do that. Then I decided to go to a bar one night, and because I'm apparently stupid and didn't think anything through, I threw myself at a guy and went home with him. Fast forward a few months, and I'm in an OB exam room talking with my doctor about who will be in the room when I give birth.

"I don't have any family here; the father isn't in the picture and I haven't really made any friends since I moved. Well, aside from a few work acquaintances. Chloe would probably be the only one I'd want in the room with me," I answer honestly. I've not had much time to make friends and the ones I did happen to hit it off with were on completely different paths in their life and didn't need a pregnant friend holding them back. They were ready to party, and enjoy their 20s. I, on the other hand, now have to be responsible and think about someone other than myself from now on. Chloe being the exception. She's not once treated me any different since finding out about my baby, if anything she's the only person I lean on.

Dr. Tucker doesn't say anything else; she just smiles at me as she finishes writing in my chart. I'm not even sure if

I want to know what she's writing, she has to think I'm pathetic.

"Well, you'll have me, Tessa. If I don't have any appointments, I'll stay with you as long as I can before delivery and after." She places a hand on my shoulder and squeezes gently. "I'll let you get out of here now, and I'll see you again in two weeks unless this little one has another plan." She smiles before she exits the room.

I move quickly to exit the room and make my way to the checkout counter to schedule my next appointment. Dealing with this girl ruins my entire appointment each time. Vivian can kiss my ass. There go those hormones again, but really, I'm not sure I'd even like *Vivian* if I wasn't a hormonal, crazy lady at the moment. Actually, I know I wouldn't like her.

I step up to the counter and hand her the sheet Dr. Tucker gave me to check out. It explains when I should return for my next appointment.

"How about June 8th? 2PM?" Vivian smiles, even her stupid smile makes me want to throw a pencil at her. I nod in agreement not trusting my words right now, especially since our last run in at the boutique. She starts writing the date and time on a small card while I enter it into my phone also. I'm the world's worst at remembering appointments and it seems pregnancy brain only makes that mishap worse.

"So, I'm assuming you probably won't have a baby shower, then right?" she says, and I pause what I'm doing to look at her. Before I can answer she continues. "Since you don't know the father, there probably won't be many to celebrate with you."

That bitch. I've had it. These are the comments that

make me so furious. I'm just about to rip her a new one in the middle of the doctor's office, when I hear a smooth voice from behind me.

"Hey, Viv. Doc in?" My core clenches as my mouth slams shut. What the hell? Without even looking, I can tell he has a face to match the sexy voice. Judging by Vivian's drool she's wiping from her mouth, my thoughts are spot on.

"Yes, she should be in her office, Kyle." Vivian's voice raises to a slutty level of purring. I watch as she winks at him. While leaning across the counter to hand me my appointment card, she uses her arms to push her boobs together. It's clear to anyone in the room what she is attempting to do here. "Did your schedule ever free up?"

"Afraid not, baby. Soon though." Well, she just got shut down and by the sounds of it, it's not the first time. Attempting to hide my shit eating grin, I thank her for the card and remove my purse from the counter. As I'm turning, the man steps to the counter beside me. I open my purse quickly and throw everything inside as I try to step aside.

"Hey." I turn at the sound of his voice being directed towards me, and I'm greeted with the darkest blue eyes. Those same blue eyes that stared down at me eight months ago. "What are you doing here?"

My purse falls to the ground, and everything inside tumbles out. I'm frozen in place momentarily, before I hear Vivian call me a clutz and I gain my composure and drop to the floor to gather my things.

Well, I drop to the floor the best I can with this belly. He drops beside me and helps gather a few things and hands them to me. I slowly stand and shove my purse over my shoulder.

I'm standing face-to-face, with my one-night stand, in my OBGYNs office. His eyes slowly move from mine down to my swollen belly. Fuck me.

*Oh, he did. Let's not forget that part.*

# 11

## KYLE

Damn.

I haven't seen her since she rode me like a damn racing stallion, then took off while I was asleep. I expected to wake up for a second round the next morning, it was *that* good. She's crossed my mind. I don't know how many times since that night. Hoping she'd walk through the entrance of my bar, but she never did.

Except now, she looks nothing like that girl. Her hips are a little wider, her face is slightly swollen in a sexy as hell way, her boobs are about double their original size. All of that's fan-fucking-tastic, including the pregnant belly she's sporting on the front. It works for her. She's fucking sexy. I've never been one to be attracted to pregnant women. Typically, they have someone tied to them and that seems like a hell of a lot of trouble, so it's never worked for me. But with Tessa, well I can totally work with it. I look behind her, expecting to see the baby's father, but she seems to be alone.

That's a dick move on his part. If I had a kid on the

way, no way in hell would I be missing any of these appointments. I've heard my sister talk enough to know that; one, women want the father there, two, you learn a lot at each appointment, and three, the woman will never let you forget how many you missed.

"Hi." She tucks a strand of her long blonde hair behind her ear. "H-how have you been?" I suddenly remember her stuttering slightly when we got back to my place that night. I figure it's a nervous habit she has. I'm still pissed about waking up alone the next morning, but choose not to bring it up. My sister's office doesn't seem to be the best place to do that, especially considering the situation she's currently in.

"Kyle," I laugh. "My names Kyle, although I'm not sure we made it that far that night, we were both pretty in the wind." He pauses before adding, "And I'm good." I shove a hand through my hair and shift on my feet, she makes me nervous and I'm not sure why. Typically, I'm a cocky bastard. Nah, cocky isn't the right word. Confident is more like it. I know what kind of face I have, the ladies in the bar remind me daily and my body is the product of years spent in the gym. "You look great..." I trail off, realizing that I don't know what to call her.

"Tessa." She smiles shyly at me. I check her out once more and notice a blush creep up the side of her neck as she watches me. Damn, I'm getting turned on by a pregnant chick in the doctor's office. Sorry, to whoever's baby mama she is. I silently pray to the brother gods.

"How far along are you?" I ask.

"Thirty-two weeks today." She grabs her keys from her purse then tosses it over her shoulder.

"Agh, not much longer," I say.

Her head tilts to the side and her brows draw together. She can't believe I know anything about pregnant chicks. Hell, it surprises anyone I come in contact with until I explain who my sister is.

"I know how long women are supposed to be pregnant," I laugh. It catches her off guard, and a small giggle escapes before she quickly turns her face back to a blank expression.

"Well, it was nice to see you again, *Kyle*." She stresses my name this time. She turns her attention back to Viv and offers a polite "thank you" before heading towards the exit. I zero in on the way her hips sway as she leaves. Damn. Now I remember what attracted me to her at the bar.

"It's sad," Viv's voice shakes me out of my trance. As I turn to look at her, her upper lip is curved into a nasty snarl. Her voice now filled with venom rather than the god-awful cat noise from earlier. "She doesn't even know who the father is. How embarrassing." I let the words sink in. The bitch just broke all the HIPPA laws, but she doesn't care. Any chance to make someone else look bad, Viv will take the shot. It's one of the reasons I'll never go out with her.

She doesn't know who the father is? She didn't strike me as that type of person, but I only spent a few hours with her, and it wasn't like we got personal during our time together.

Besides, I can't really judge anything about this girl considering our night together was a one night stand that started out in a bar.

"Quit checking out my patients, you little perv." My sister comes up behind me and slaps the back of my head. I turn on my heel so I'm facing her. Anytime my mother or sister is around, my poor head takes a beating. The women in my life are always quick to tell me what a tool I am, or call me out on my shit.

My sister is tall. We share the same blue eyes, but our hair color is the polar opposite. She has dad's blonde hair while I have mom's black hair.

I roll my eyes. "I wasn't." I give her the biggest shit-eating grin I can manage. Although, she can see right through it.

"You know, it'd be nice to see you more than once a month. I miss you." She nudges my arm. I rarely see my sister, and I know it's something I need to fix. She's the only sibling I have, and I truly do love her. I just can't stand that douchebag she's with. He's an asshole, and as independent and strong willed as my sister is, I can't figure out why she is still with someone like him.

"I miss you, too, Lou. You know how it is, I've got things going on." I wave my hand dramatically in the air, then quickly lean in and place a kiss against her cheeks.

"Yeah, with that little sports bar of yours," she teases. She knows my bar is one of the most popular places in the city right now and is packed at least five nights a week. "Besides, if I can find time in my schedule to have lunch with you, surely you can find time in yours for your big sis." She crosses her arms in a challenge. I fold, there's no use in fighting her.

"You're right, your schedule is a hell of a lot crazier than mine. You never know when you have to work." I offer her my arm. "You ready?"

She tosses her white coat on the hook and links her arm with mine. I begin leading her towards the exit.

"See ya, Viv." I give her a wink. God. I'm an awful

human being, but she's so easy to tease. My sister makes a gagging noise and I chuckle as we walk towards the door.

"So, how's everything going?" I ask as we sit at a small diner down the street from her office. We've ordered drinks and an appetizer.

"It's going." She shrugs her shoulders, it's her way of putting off the truth. Something is bothering her, and as her brother I will make it my mission to get it out of her.

"Just going?" I ask, raising my brows. She sits back in her seat, blowing a deep breath out and crossing her arms. "How's your boyfriend?"

"Good." That one word reply let's me know that it's getting worse between the two of them. They've been dating for nearly six years, they've lived together for two. She didn't want to move in together until she finished her residency.

She's miserable, I can see it. Hell, everyone can see it. I've watched my sister go from being a happy, always giggling, living life to the fullest person, to this woman in front of me that I hardly recognize. Her pain is deep, it shows.

"Just good?" I cross my arms, laying my elbows on the table in front of me. "Cut the shit, Lou. Tell me what's going on."

"I'm just–" she pauses. "It's just–" She looks up at me, I'm patient waiting for her reply. I can see she's struggling with this and it makes me mad. "Peter has just been an ass lately." I huff as she continues. "Even more of an ass than usual." She rolls her eyes.

"What's he doing?" I ask.

"He's just always picking fights. Nothing is good enough, I work too much, I'm never home, I don't show him enough affection." I see the tears starting to form in her eyes. "I'm just not good enough anymore basically." She shrugs her shoulders, trying to brush it off like it isn't gutting her right now.

"You know that's bullshit. You're perfect, Lou. Being an obstetrician was always your dream, he knew that when the two of you got together." I remind her. She doesn't say anything so I continue. "Are you still happy?" She shrugs her shoulders, but doesn't offer a reply. "What does that mean?"

"I'm not sure. Some days I think about leaving and then others I feel like I'd be throwing a huge part of my life away. It's scary, and I'm just not sure if that's the right choice."

"I get it. It's a lot of change, but sis, if things just continue to get worse what are you going to do?"

"I don't know." She looks up at me, her face is pale. "I kind of think he may be cheating on me." That floors me and was not at all what I was expecting her to say.

"W-what?" I barely get the word out. I'm so shocked. He's a tool, for-sure, but I didn't think he was a cheater. My hands ball into fists without even realizing it, until she puts her hand on mine.

"He's always complaining about me working later, but the past week or so he's kind of encouraged it but he still has a piss poor attitude about it." Our drinks and appetizer comes, she waits to continue when the waitress has left our table. "The other day, I made it a point to come home early. I kept thinking to myself that I needed to work on our relationship, and if me working so late was an issue then that was something I could begin working on. I could just schedule my clients earlier in the day and they would have to be compliant with it. So, I brought dinner home from his favorite restaurant, to try to mend what's broken between us. He didn't even thank me."

I nod, popping a chip into my mouth as she speaks.

"Well, he was on the couch when I walked in. It was just odd." she says as she takes a chip and dips it into the salsa before taking a bite. "He jumped. He was so shocked that I was home, I laughed it off at first but then when I was laying in bed that night I started thinking about how he was quick to put his phone up. Almost like he was doing something he shouldn't, each time he got it out the rest of the night he would turn the screen so I couldn't see, or click off whatever it was when I'd walk by."

"That does seem shady." Exactly what a cheating motherfucker would do.

"That night that I came home early, he stayed up late. Later than he normally does. We didn't even spend any time together, barely even spoke to one another." She shrugs her shoulders, trying to downplay her emotions. "I went to bed by ten and he was gone before I woke up."

"What makes you think he's cheating?" I ask.

"He's just distant. Something is going on, it may not be cheating. But something is definitely going on." I completely agree with her.

"I'm sorry, Lou."

"I'll be okay." She waves her hand at me and gets another chip. I watch her as she eats, this is breaking my sister and that's the one thing that pisses me off the most. "So, tell me. What's been going on with you?"

"Nothing much." I shrug my shoulders, and my mind wanders to Tessa. "I've been staying busy."

"I know this, I never see my brother anymore. Have

you seen mom and dad?" I nod, popping a chip into my mouth.

"Yeah, dad and I rode bikes the other day." I look at my sister, there's a sadness in her eyes that won't go away no matter what we talk about. "You okay?"

"Yeah, I'll be fine." She half smiles and it guts me. I'm going to have to talk to her shit head boyfriend about all this.

We spend the rest of our lunch talking about Tessa and how I knew her. I leave out all the details of our night together, only admitting to knowing her from the bar.

# 12

## TESSA

KYLE WAS the last person I expected to see, and especially in my OBGYNs office. Of all the places, it just had to be there? I imagined running into him in Target, or the market. Hell, maybe even the coffee shop, or Disney World. But the OB's office?

What in the hell have I done to deserve this kind of karma?

And damn him to hell, if he didn't look sexy as shit standing there. His faded jeans were hanging low on his hips and his shirt stretched across his sculpted chest. I honestly thought guys only looked like him in movies or books, and the sex that night? A-fucking-mazing!

Thankfully, he didn't put two and two together in the doctor's office and cause a scene. I'd always told myself if I ran into him, I'd lay everything out on the table. I just hoped it would have been an appropriate place, and seeing him in my doctor's office caught me off guard, and I wasn't sure what to say to him. I mean was I supposed to just blurt out that I was pregnant with his baby?

I wanted to ask for his number, but he was clearly there to see the doctor and was way too busy flirting with *Vivian* of all people. The whore.

I was so shocked by running into him. I wasn't thinking clearly, or I would have forced myself to set up a time to talk with him. But then the fear of rejection would have sent me spiraling out of control with nervousness and each scenario I play out in my head doesn't end well.

"Ugh." I groan, as I slam the bathroom door in my apartment. I have no ties to this man, so I don't know why the two of them flirting royally pisses me off. Well, except for the obvious tie. I look down at my belly and run my hand across it slowly.

Why does it bother me so badly that she kept trying to free up his schedule?

I shower and head straight for my bed. I should be working on a few listings I have going up for sale, but I find myself instead searching random Kyles on Facebook. I'm not even sure what my plan is, if I happen to run across him.

I would private message him, but then what would I say?

*'Hey Kyle, remember me? I'm the chick from that one-night stand nearly eight months ago? Oh btw, I'm pregnant and you're the daddy?'*

Yeah, that sounds like a winner. I slap a palm to my forehead, what a nightmare.

Eventually, I give up and shut my laptop. I'll deal with this another day.

# 13

# KYLE

I'M glad I was finally able to have lunch with my sister. We usually can't go very far because of her afternoon appointments, and she is typically always on call in case of a labor emergency. I really do admire my big sister for her hard work ethics, she cares about her patients a lot, and it shows in her work.

Eventually, she drilled me the entire time about Tessa and how I knew her. So, I semi told her the truth. I met her at the bar a while ago. I just happen to leave out the parts about the unbelievable sex or how she left me stranded the next morning. God, that still pisses me off. And for the record, withholding information isn't lying.

I want to call that dickhead of a boyfriend and figure out what the hell is going on. I can't stand seeing my sister like this, she's struggling and I know she didn't tell me everything that's been going on.

After we ate, I dropped Lou off outside her building, not wanting to chance another run in with Viv. That girl struggles with taking a hint, but I don't make it easy on her either, which is why I only go into my sister's office when I'm picking her up for a lunch date. She hits on me every single time I step foot inside and it always pisses my sister off when Viv asks about me constantly. That's really why I keep teasing her. What kind of little brother would I be if I didn't annoy my sister at every opportunity I got? A shitty one, that's what kind and I refuse to give sweet ole Lou a shitty brother, I just don't have it in me.

Driving back to my place, my mind keeps wandering back to Tessa. Damn, she looked good today. Pregnant or not. Watching her walk out of the office, with those hips swaying almost made me go after her. I almost regret not chasing her down. Maybe for a quick catch up. And, already thirty-two weeks.

Hell, come to think of it, it's been about eight months since I last saw her. She must have gotten pregnant right around the time we hooked up. My blood starts to boil thinking about her hooking up with someone so soon after her hook up to me, but I tamp it down. I have no reason to get jealous of her, I've met the girl once.

I pull into my driveway and throw the truck into park. My neighborhood is quiet during the afternoon, the street usually isn't occupied during the day like this.

I flip the sun visor down to look in the mirror before hopping out of my truck. Thoughts of Tessa and the way her ass looked in my sister's office today run through my mind, followed by our night together.

Wait. A. Damn. Minute.

It can't be. No. I start calculating the time since our night together.

I know exactly who the fucking father of Tessa's baby is.

I'm looking at him.

*Fuck,* It's me.

# 14

# KYLE

BY THE TIME I'm dialing my sister's number, it's late. I've spend the rest of the time thinking about what to say or how to handle this situation.

"Kyle? Everything oka-"

"No, everything is not fucking ok." I cut her off not letting her get a word in. I slam my front door shut behind me. So much for a quiet neighborhood today, folks. "I need Tessa's number. *Now*." My voice is harsher than I intended it to be.

"Kyle. Calm down. You know I can't give out patients information like that," she sighs into the phone. "That's confidential, not to mention a HIPPA violation and I could lose my license. What has gotten into you and why the hell are you talking to me this way?" She's getting angry now and I know this conversation will get us nowhere if we are both going at each other's throats.

"Lou," I yell into the phone. "I need you to be my sister right now and get me her number." I can feel the anger radiating off of me.

Why didn't she tell me? Why hasn't she tried finding me? As far as I know, she has never returned to the bar. I would have seen her. I know I would have noticed her. It would be impossible not to.

"What the hell is wrong with you, Kyle?" My sister barks through the phone. How in the hell do you explain something like this?

"I need her number. I think she may be pregnant with my baby." I grunt. I can't believe this is happening. This actually can't be happening. I don't know the first thing about being a father, hell I'm not mature enough to be a father. I'm still killing it at the bachelor life and I actually like it. I'm good at it.

"Are you fucking kidding me?" My sister shouts through the phone. I can hear her dickhead of a boyfriend telling her to be quiet in the background. Fucking asshole.

Lou and I chat for the next few minutes. Arguing is a better suited description. Followed by having her yell at my ass for a few more minutes for knocking up a girl in a drunken state.

"You know, I'm actually surprised that this hasn't happened before now, truthfully." She scolds me, and I feel like I did all those times mom had to chew my ass a new one for doing something stupid. Making me feel all but about two foot tall. Something both the women in my life are really good at doing when I need it.

"That was a cheap shot."

"Well, hell Kyle. It's true." She's pissed, but not as pissed as I am. I can hear Peter saying something in the background. "It's my brother." She says to him, her tone has change. "I'm not getting off the phone."

"What the hell is he bitching about?" I ask her.

"Nothing." She's short. "Dammit, Kyle. You've put me in a difficult situation."

Eventually, Lou sends me a text with Tessa's phone number and tells me to proceed with caution. I realize my sister is breaking so many different laws by doing this, but I don't know what else to do here. I can't hang out at her office like a stalker waiting on her. Really, I can't imagine having to spend that much time with Viv, nor would Lou allow me to cause a scene in the practice she has worked her ass off to create.

My sister tells me that Tessa doesn't have anyone in the city with her, so she's virtually alone and has been doing everything by herself.

Now, I feel like a jackass for not knowing. But she could have told me at the office today instead of just letting me watch her ass walk to the door. Literally.

I dial her number eight times before I click it off and toss it on the couch beside me.

How do I approach this situation without screwing it all up?

I grab my phone and open a new text. My fingers hover over the keys trying to find the right words.

> Hey Tessa. It's Kyle. You busy?

I press send and wait a few minutes. My screen is black with no new messages. I'm starting to sweat. I'm so damn nervous about the response when my phone finally dings.

> Hi. Not really. How'd you get my number?

I forced Lou to give it to me. Don't be mad at her.

Tessa: Lou?

Your doctor.

You're on a first name basis with my OBGYN?

I am when she's my sister.

Of course, she is…

I need to talk to you.

I wait. And wait.

Please? Can I meet you for breakfast tomorrow?

Sure. I have something to tell you anyways. How about the bakery on twelfth? Seven-thirty-ish?

Got it. It's a date.

Suddenly, I'm scared shitless. Thinking and hearing you're going to be a father are two totally different things. Tomorrow morning, my future is going to change. I just have to decide how to deal with it.

# 15

# TESSA

I WAKE up not at all rested as I had hoped I'd be. Sleep doesn't come easy these days anyways, add that to my nerves about telling Kyle he's going to be a father in less than a month, and I have been sick to my stomach. I've been forced to run to the bathroom several times. How am I going to tell Kyle this news that will change his life forever?

*Oh, hey Kyle. How are ya? Long time no see, yeah I'm good just pregnant with your baby. Every man's dream, I'm sure.*

I roll my eyes. This cannot be happening.

I pull into the parking lot of the bakery and find a parking spot close to the exit. I may need a quick escape after this one. After shutting the car off, I can't seem to move. I'm just staring at my steering wheel hoping my car will miraculously start itself and drive me home. I'm not at all prepared for this, prepared to now have another being in this baby's life.

Oh God, what if Kyle doesn't actually want anything to

do with the baby? I haven't thought this through. Maybe I should just run away and save us all the heartache.

Before I have a chance to overthink the situation even more than I already have, I force myself to get out of the car.

I start to open my car door just as I see Kyle climbing out of his truck. It's a black F150 that stands way too tall for me to comfortably climb in and out of but somehow, he climbs out with ease. Damn him.

I watch for what seems like hours as he takes the ball cap from his head and tosses it to the dashboard of the truck and runs a hand through his messy hair. *His perfect messy hair.* Ok Tessa, get it together. You're drooling in a bakery parking lot before eight o'clock in the morning over a man you had a one night fuck with. I giggle to myself at that one, how pathetic am I. Knocked up after a one-night stand to a man that looks like sex on a stick.

Ugh. Damn the luck.

Oh, how the gossip mills back home would be working overtime with this story.

Just as I shut my car door, Kyle turns, and our eyes connect. In that moment, I'm damn near sure he knows the secret I have to tell him. His eyes burn into mine making the hairs on my arms stand to attention and a chill creeps down my spine.

He makes his way to my car, "Good morning." He smiles sweetly at me, but his jaw ticks in the process.

"Good morning," I repeat. I quickly advert my attention toward the front of the bakery needing an escape from all this tension. "Shall we?"

Kyle places his hand on the small of my back guiding me towards the entrance. The feel of his hand on me makes me aware of how close he is. I can smell his cologne, it's the same smell he had that night in the bar.

I reach for the handle, but he's quicker and beats me to it, opening the door wide as I step through. The bakery is fairly packed this morning with only a few open tables, one in the far back and one beside the entrance door. I make my way towards the one closest to us thinking it'll make for an easy escape if this conversation goes south, but I'm stopped short when Kyle grabs my hand and pulls me to the rear of the building. *Damn all the luck.*

I sit in the chair he's pulled out for me and quickly toss my purse into the extra seat beside me. He moves around the table and sits directly across from me.

"What would you like, and I'll go order?" Kyle asks, staring into my eyes once more. He makes me nervous when he stares at me this way, it's intense.

"A coffee is fine, decaf. And a blueberry muffin." He walks towards the ordering station leaving me to my thoughts once again on how I'll be able to tell this man he will be a father in a very short amount of time.

Kyle returns after ordering our drinks and pastries, I watch as he folds his large frame into the tiny table we are occupying.

"So, how've you been?" He folds his hands together and I'm drawn to the action. I remember those hands... STOP THIS TESSA! My god, you're a horny heifer.

"I've been good. You?" I bite my bottom lip nervously, waiting for his response.

"Busy. The bar has picked up its pace quite a bit lately, I haven't had much time off."

"Oh, I didn't realize you worked that often." I'm an idiot. Of course, he works insane hours. He's a bartender.

"No, Tessa. I *own* the bar." He does a little laugh that causes me to clench my thighs together.

*What a sound.*

"Oh. I had no idea." Our coffee and pastries are delivered before I can continue. I happily use my coffee as my escape from conversation for as long as I can.

"What do you do for a living?" He takes a bite of his donut and I'm drawn to the way his tongue darts out and touches his lips. I glance to his eyes to realize he's caught me watching and I immediately blush a million shades of red. Not fifty, but a million.

"I'm a real estate agent. I work from home mostly." Damn hormones almost made me stutter.

"That'll be great once the baby is born, right?" He leans forward on his elbows engrossed in what I'm about to say.

"Yeah, I suppose." His question about the baby causes me to lose my focus. I need to just rip the band aid off so to speak, I've never wanted the baby to not have a father and if Kyle chooses not to be in the picture then I've done my part. I was never going to hide the baby from him. Here goes nothing.

"Speaking of the baby..." I trail off and put my focus back on his face. "There is something I need to tell you."

"I already know." He leans back in his chair, once again looking good enough to eat. He has such a calm demeanor about him, one that only attracts me more to him. "That's why I asked you here, actually. I know the baby is mine." I gasp at his words, completely taken off guard.

I'm sure the look on my face at this moment is very similar to the look of a deer stuck in bright headlights. My heart is pounding, my ears are ringing, I'm suddenly falling and then everything goes black.

# 16

## KYLE

"Lou," I say my sister's name with an urgency, I'm not used to hearing in my voice.

"Kyle? What is it? It's eight-fifteen on a Saturday morning."

"It's Tessa. Sh-shes.." I concentrate on turning behind the ambulance that is holding Tessa in the back unconscious.

"What's wrong with her? Where are you?" She's panicking now.

"She's being transported to the hospital by ambulance. She passed out in the bakery this morning. I'm following them now," I sigh. I've never felt so scared than when she started falling out of her chair. Her face had flushed, and her head lolled to the side, I knocked the table over in the process of catching her before she hit the ground completely. "I need you, Lou." My voice breaks when I cry to my sister.

"I'm on my way." I can already hear her garage door opening and the dinging of the car, telling me she's already climbing inside. "I'll be right there, Kyle. Concentrate on driving, we don't need both of you in the hospital." My sister ends the call and I toss my phone into the cup holder of my console. The paramedics wouldn't allow me to ride with her due to space in the back and them needing room to work on her. I wanted to argue, but knew I'd get nowhere if I did.

We pull up at the emergency entrance of the hospital and I don't even bother parking my truck, let them tow it. I don't give a shit. I just need to get to Tessa and make sure they're both going to be ok.

I'm at the back of the rig door before they even have her out. She's still unconscious, laying on the gurney as they wheel her out. She's a ghostly, pale color and my heart rate doubles in fear.

"What's wrong with her?" I shout.

A paramedic places his hand on my chest pushing me away from them all, "Sir. Sir!" I shove his hand away and try to get around him. He wraps his arms around me, holding me in place. "I need you to stay calm. We are doing everything we can to help her, but we need you to stay out of the way and allow us to do our jobs."

"Kyle." I hear my sister's voice. She's exiting the doors they are wheeling Tessa towards. "I've got her." My sister takes the chart from the paramedic's hands and follows them inside. I follow dumbly unsure what to do or where to go from here. The paramedics are telling Lou about Tessa's condition and her blood pressure, but I can't understand a word they are saying because all I can see is the girl laying on the stretcher as they roll her through the doors.

"Sir," an older lady calls out to me. She rounds the front desk and makes her way towards me, grabbing a pen from the desk in the process. She is holding a clip board with some paperwork attached to it. "Sir. Hi. I'm Margaret." She has a friendly smile. "I'm the receptionist here, can you please fill out these papers while you wait for an update? Standard questions, such as info and insurance." She steps beside me and begins flipping through the papers. "You will just need to sign here and here and initial the other pages."

I stare down at the paperwork. Sick to my stomach. I realize I know nothing about her. Not her last name, not her birth date, or address. Not her due date or the name of our unborn child.

"I don't know any of this information." I grip the clipboard in my hand.

"Oh, I'm sorry. I just assumed you were the father." She walks back behind her desk leaving me standing in the middle of a waiting room feeling like a complete jackass for not knowing anything about my child or my child's mother.

"I am," I whisper, before collapsing in a chair in the waiting room.

# 17

## KYLE

IT'S BEEN two hours since Lou went behind the double doors with Tessa. No one has given me an update. Dad sent a text to let me know that he and my mom are both on their way here now. I'm assuming Lou called our mom and filled her in on everything that has transpired over the last twenty-four hours.

*Shit.* The bar.

I pull my phone from my pocket and fire off a quick text to Tony, letting him know that I won't be in for a couple of days I'm sure. His reply is almost instant.

> I've got it covered. Everything okay?

> Yeah, long story. I'll explain later.

> Sounds good, boss.

"Ugh." I rub my hands over my face, with frustration. I hate not knowing what is going on in situations like this, plus the fact that I'll have to explain everything to my parents shortly.

I've sat in this waiting room, in the same spot the entire two hours afraid I'll miss something if I move. The room is quiet with a few TVs playing different channels, but I'm not focused on them.

My gaze slides to the other occupants of the waiting room. One woman is wearing a mask over her face that covers a nasty cough she seems to be battling. Another woman has her toddler laying across her lap, he obviously doesn't feel good. The woman rocks an infant seat sitting on the floor beside her chair, a little baby snoozes away inside.

"Son." I hear my dad's voice as he enters the sliding door. I look up just as they both find me and rush to me. I stand as my parents engulf me into a hug, and for the first time, I relax. "Any updates?" I hadn't realized how much I needed someone with me until I felt their arms wrap around me.

"Not yet. No one knows anything." My mother takes my hands and motions for us to sit.

"Tell me about Tessa. I want to know everything." She smiles, a smile that says she isn't judging and just truly wants to know.

"I don't really have much to tell you, and that makes me feel like an ass, Ma."

"Language," she warns, and I almost laugh. I've been cursing in front of her since I was a toddler, at least that is what my pops says. Every time she attempts to get onto me by reminding me of the language I'm using.

"It's true, though. I know nothing about Tessa other than she is eight months pregnant with a child we created on a drunken night at the bar, and she's a real estate agent and your daughter is her OBGYN."

My dad places his arm across my back, reassuring me that everything will be alright. Just then, the double doors to the surgery wing open and my sister walks out, blood smeared across her coat. Oh, God.

"Lou." I push away from mom and dad and meet my sister halfway across the waiting room.

"Kyle." She grabs my shoulders and urges me back towards the seating area. "I need you to sit down. I have a lot to explain to you."

I do as she says, my stomach bottoming out. I know she's going to tell me I've lost one of them. I can feel it.

"Tessa typically has extremely high blood pressure. Her blood pressure has run on the high side for most of her pregnancy, but nothing we haven't been able to maintain control of. However, today it shot up dangerously high for both her and the infant which is what caused her to black out this morning when she bottomed out. She is fine now and resting. The baby is doing great, too."

I'm up and out of my chair heading for the double doors. I need to see her with my own eyes to know that she's going to be okay.

"Kyle!" she yells. "Kyle! You cannot go back yet. She needs to rest and you being there right now is a lot." I hear my sister, but I'm not comprehending what she is saying. I need to find Tessa. She is alone right now. I need to be with her. "Kyle, dammit STOP!" my sister yells down the hall, and it causes me to pause. I turn to look at her. She has anger and sadness in her eyes.

"What, Lou?" I wait for her to catch up to me. "I need

to get to her, she's alone." My parents come crashing through the double doors behind her.

"Just let me explain everything first." I glance down at the blood coating her white jacket and clothes. My sisters' eyes follow mine and she shakes her head when her gaze meets mine again. "It's not as bad as it seems. She hit her head on the corner of the table when she fell, it's a superficial wound. No damage, she just has a few stitches."

A breath I hadn't even realized I'd been holding releases from my chest. My lungs fill with air again and it burns. I was so terrified during the entire ordeal I didn't even realize she hit her head before I shoved the table out of the way.

"Can I please go to her now?" My mother is wrapping me in her arms, but I don't return the hug. I just need to focus on the two of them right now. I wasn't sure how I'd react to becoming a father. I sure didn't believe I'd have this natural instinct to protect, especially not both of them.

"I'll send Dr. Kirk out to get you." She smiles at me before disappearing back into the hallway and the doors swallow her up.

"Mom, what the fuck am I going to do? I don't know how to do any of this." I wrap my arms around my mother's neck as she rubs my back, reassuring me everything will work out the way it should.

Once we are seated in the waiting room again, we patiently wait for Dr. Kirk to bring us back and update us on their status. I tell my parents everything. I tell them how she caught my attention that night in the bar and how I didn't even get her name or number that night, but I really planned to. She had just left before I had gotten the chance to. They ask about my plan now that I've learned of the pregnancy and I'm unsure how to answer. I'm not sure what Tessa wants, really. We never made it that far this morning.

"Mr. Tucker?" An older man stands at the double doors in a set of scrubs. I stand, pulling his attention to me. "I'm Dr. Kirk. I understand you'd like to see your wife." He smiles and reaches his hand out between us, I take it. I should correct him that Tessa isn't my wife, but I don't. Following him towards the double doors he says, "Your parents are welcome to join." He holds the door open and I turn to face my parents. I don't think Tessa would enjoy meeting her child's grandparents in a situation like this. Before I have a chance to tell them my plans, they graciously explain that they're going to grab some lunch and will call me later for details.

# 18

## KYLE

I FOLLOW Dr. Kirk down a long hall. Hospital halls creep me out. Doors are always open, and you can stare right into someone's room as you're passing. Awkward eye contact and all.

We pass several rooms before he finally slows and presses against a door before entering.

"Hello, Tessa," he says, as he moves around to the foot of the bed. She looks pale still, not the vibrant glow she had this morning. She has a bandage wrapped around her head and her hospital gown is falling off one of her shoulders. I stare at her while the doctor speaks, I'm not paying attention to what he's saying, and I know I should be. All I can think of is how scared I was when she fell. I don't think I've ever had a moment like that in my life.

Now I'm staring at her and she is ok. They are telling me she is ok. Then I just feel guilty that she has had to deal with things like this the entire pregnancy and she hasn't had anyone to lean on for the past eight months. That's rough.

"If you have any questions, please let me know. Someone should be in shortly with discharge information, I'd like for you to stay the night so we can monitor your blood pressure, but unfortunately, there is nothing I can do if you'd rather leave." He nods his head and then moves towards where I'm standing to exit the room.

I nod at him as he passes.

"Hi," Tessa says, in a voice so soft I almost didn't hear it.

"How are you feeling?" I ask, as I move towards the bed. I'm unsure of what my role here is so I remain standing a good distance away.

"I've been better." She attempts to laugh, but the movement causes her to grab her head in pain. "I guess we have a lot to talk about, huh?" She smiles, and I can't help but smile myself.

"I guess we do." And she's right. We need to get everything out in the open if we are going to make this all work. "I didn't know," I say, as I pull a seat up next to her bed. "I didn't know, or I would have been here all along." I rest my elbows on my knees and run my hands over my face. It's an act I do when I'm nervous and stressed.

"I came to the bar," she says, and I freeze. "I came looking for you." I look at her, glancing back and forth between her eyes. "You weren't there. I spoke with Tony, but he didn't remember me and basically told me you aren't interested in more than one night." I watch as a tear slides down her cheek, I instinctively reach out and wipe the tear with the pad of my thumb.

"What?" I look at her and my heart is breaking. I grab her hand in mine. "I wanted to get your number; I had made up my mind that only one night with you wasn't an option for me. When I woke up the next morning, you were already gone so I never got the chance."

# 19

# TESSA

KYLE INSISTS on driving me from the hospital to my apartment. I assured him I felt fine after the fall, but he wouldn't take no for an answer.

It's odd having him in my space. This space seems smaller with his large presence in it. I drop my purse off beside the door as I toe my shoes off. I'm exhausted from the events of the day and thankful I was able to persuade them into letting me come home today, instead of staying the night in an uncomfortable hospital bed with staff in and out all night long.

I grab some bottles of water from the fridge and move towards my small living room. My apartment is modest, but I love it. It has hardwood flooring throughout that gives the perfect contrast to the white walls. I have minimal furniture since it is so small, but I've made the space work for me and I'm really proud of it all.

I didn't grow up with much, so I've worked hard for everything I have. My mom died when I was little, and my father turned his attention to alcohol instead of focusing on his daughter. Shortly after, I was removed from his care and placed in a foster home. My father never contacted me, never showed up for court. I eventually aged out of the system and took off as soon as I figured my shit out.

Becoming a real estate agent wasn't the top of my list of career choices, but I really do enjoy it and it gives me some freedom with my schedule, which I love. Not to mention, the pay isn't bad either.

Handing Kyle the water I sit on the edge of the sofa. He's already seated and staring at me as he twists the lid to his water. I watch as he lifts the bottle to his lips and takes a large drink. His Adam's apple bobs with each swallow and I just stare, completely unaware that he's been watching me, watch him.

His throat clears and I jump. I can feel the blush creep up my neck as the heat floods my face. Horny freaking heifer.

"Sorry." I smile. "So, let's just get this over with."

Kyle leans forward, placing the water on the coffee table in front of him before he turns his attention to me, resting his elbows on his knees. He looks sexy as hell when he does that and I'm not sure if I'll be able to concentrate on the conversation with those eyes on me.

"So, the baby," he starts. "I know I'm the father." I nod to his statement. I expected some anger or something, but he's calm as he says it.

"Yes." I pause waiting to see if he will say anything else. "We can have a paternity test done once he is born," I rush out. I can't blame him for feeling the baby possibly couldn't be his after only one night together. He doesn't know he is the only one I've been with for years.

"No, I believe you. No need for a-" He stops suddenly

and his eyes jerk to mine. "Wait, did you say *he?*" His lips twitch like he's trying not to smile.

"Yes, I just found out last month that the baby is a boy." I place my hand over my stomach and rub gently. This always stirs him up and gets him to kicking and I love the feeling.

"Wow." He shakes his head in disbelief. "We're having a boy," he says, and I smile at the joy in his tone. My shoulders relax slightly once I realize that he isn't angry.

"So, you want to be involved then?" I throw the question out, before I'm able to second guess it.

"Absolutely. I'd never abandon my child, Tessa. Always remember that. Regardless of the situation with you and I, you are his mother and I am his father and that will always stay the same."

I'm relieved to hear him say he wants to be a part of it all. I was worried he'd decide not to be a part of this all. Especially, given the circumstances.

The baby kicks and it hurts slightly.

"Ouch." I grab the spot and bend slightly.

"What is it? What's wrong?" Kyle is in front of me in seconds.

"Nothing. Sorry I shouldn't have scared you, he just kicked." I smile at him.

"Can I?" he asks. I grab his hand and slowly press it against the side of my swollen belly and rub. Just as I predicted, the baby begins kicking and the smile on Kyle's face when he finally feels his son is one that I won't ever forget. The first time I ever felt the baby kick was one of the best days. I had been so nervous for weeks before that I hadn't felt anything, and my doctor kept assuring me that everything was fine, and it was normal at that stage. "Wow." A smile dances across Kyle's lips. His hand slowly begins moving on its own across my stomach, and I have to squeeze my legs together to control the feeling his touch does to me.

# 20

## TESSA

IT'S GETTING LATE ALREADY. Kyle still hasn't left; we've discussed as much as we can, but I'm exhausted from the events of the day and really just want to crawl into bed and call it a day.

"It's getting late," I say to Kyle, as I light up the screen on my phone to check the time. "9:45."

"I don't feel comfortable leaving you after the day you've had." His admission startles me, but triggers something inside of me. I'm not used to having anyone care. He moves to stand, but I stop him.

"I'm sorry I didn't find you sooner." I meet his eyes. "When I went back to the bar that day, I was hopeful when I walked in. I was scared shitless, but I was determined to make sure the father knew. That *you* knew." I shrug my shoulders before continuing. "Then, the decision would have been yours. Whether you wanted to be a part of this baby's life or not.

Our eyes hold for a long while before he finally opens his mouth to speak but stops himself.

"I don't know what to say, Tessa." He shakes his head and runs his hands down the front of his face.

"It's okay." I can't help but wonder how different things would have been for me if I'd have found him that day. Would he have missed any doctor's appointments?

"I had no idea." He leans towards me and places an arm around my shoulders, resting against the couch. "I'm sorry, no one ever told me that you came by."

"I didn't recognize the kid working, but I asked for Tony and that's when he told me everything. I'm sorry I didn't insist on seeing you." I drop my head to my hands. "I was just hurt by the words and annoyed that I hadn't been able to find you."

"Don't stress about it now. That's in the past, now we need to focus on the future and what our plans are." His words put me at ease, talking about the future.

"Can we focus on it tomorrow? I'm beat." My hand moves to cover my yawn, pregnancy has made me sleep all the time and its way past the time I normally go to sleep.

"Sure. How about I stay here tonight?" His words take me off guard, staying together probably isn't the best idea considering we have so much to discuss. "I'll stay on the couch so you can wipe that goofy look off your face," he chuckles and I relax. The couch I can handle.

"Okay." I stand and retrieve a spare pillow from my bed and bring it out to him, before grabbing the blanket off the back of the couch. He kicks his shoes off as I make the couch into a bed for him. Once he's comfortable, I head to my room, and as soon as my head hits the pillow I'm drifting to sleep.

# 21

## KYLE

IT TAKES FOREVER to fall asleep. My mind keeps running over the events of the day. I was so scared when Tessa was lying on the floor, motionless. The paramedics couldn't come soon enough, and I was close to just driving her to the hospital myself.

I'm going to be a father. I don't think I've still fully grasped the idea. It's nerve wracking. There will be a tiny being that will fully depend on Tessa and I. But, I'm in this. I want my child to know who I am and know they'll always be able to count on me.

I hate the thought of Tessa having to do everything by herself the past few months while she has been pregnant. I don't even know if she has any friends here and my sister had mentioned she has no family. I really need to figure out her story.

I pull my phone from my pocket and text Lou.

Hey. You up?

I wait for my sister's reply, after a few minutes the texting bubble appears.

> Yeah. How's Tessa?

She's good, I'm staying at her place tonight.

> Kyle.

I shake my head, it's not what she's thinking. This is bigger than a quick fuck now, there's more at stake.

Chill. I'm on the couch.

> Good. So, did the two of you get a chance to talk?

Not much. We will talk more in the morning I'm sure. I just don't know how to approach the entire situation.

> Go slow. You need to remember that she has done everything by herself up until this point, so she probably won't willingly ask for help.

That's what I'm afraid of.

Admitting that isn't easy.

> I know she has a Lamaze class scheduled soon, ask her about it.

What the fuck is Lamaze?

It's the breathing class, dumbass. It's beneficial, trust me.

If you say so.

I do. Lol

I can't believe I'm going to be a dad.

You'll be a great one, don't doubt that, brother.

I'll try like hell.

Goodnight.

I open a new message to text my mom. I forgot to let them know that we were released from the hospital earlier, and I'm really shocked that she hasn't called or texted me. She probably knew I needed some time and we had a lot of shit to work out.

Hey, momma.

Hi, baby. How is Tessa?

She's good, she's asleep now.

Good. She needs her rest. Today was probably rough on her. How are you?

Soaking it all in. I can't believe I'm going to be a dad.

That thought scares the shit out of me each time it crosses my mind. I have a damn good dad, but what if I suck at it? I've been living my life as a playboy. I don't know how to do the relationship thing, but having a baby is different. I have to be there for him, or her. I just don't want to fuck it all up.

> I can't believe my baby is having a baby. Lol

I hope I am good at this.

> Give yourself some credit, son. You have a great daddy to follow.

You're right. I do.

> I was thinking earlier, and I want you to run this by Tessa to see how she feels. Lou told me she didn't really have anyone and has been doing this all on her own. So, I'd like to throw her a baby shower. If that's ok with the two of you.

I don't know, I'll ask her. I'm not sure what all she has for the baby yet; we didn't get that far in our conversation earlier. She was really tired.

> Sure, sure. Just ask her and let me know what she says. Get you some rest too, sweetheart. We love you.

Love you, too, mom.

I toss my phone onto the floor beside the couch and roll to my side to get comfortable. The thoughts of the day are on repeat in my mind, but I smile knowing what's to come.

———

MY ASS IS DRAGGING TODAY. Sleeping on Tessa's couch did not help matters. Mix that with the events of the day and I'm just shot. Stocking products at the bar is usually one of my favorite things, but I'm only running on maybe three hours of sleep. *Maybe.*

Sleep just wouldn't come last night. I kept thinking about Tessa and how scared I was. Seeing her in the hospital bed with just me there to support her. When the doctor said the baby was okay, I have never experienced relief like that before.

"Here's another box, Boss." Tony sits the create down on the bar where I'm working. He's called me Boss since he started working for me a few years ago. I've tried getting him to quit, but he always says it's what I am and that he likes it that way. I don't argue anymore, it's a waste of time with him. Tony begins pulling glasses out and placing them on the shelf under the bar, lining them up in neat rows.

"So, what happened the other day?" Tony asks. I grab another glass, holding it up to the like to make sure it's been cleaned properly.

"Well," I pause, unsure how to approach this topic with someone who is more of a best friend to me than an actual employee. "Remember a while back, a girl came into the bar. I danced with her, then we took off." He stares at me.

"Dude, that's like every night." I punch him in the shoulder. "Ouch." He rubs his hand over the spot.

"Shut the fuck up, I do not." I point out. I've struggling getting Tessa out of my head, I've been tempted and I've even tried to take a few girls home. It just wasn't anything like that night. "Anyways, me and this girl, Tess is her name." I add, feeling as if he needs to know this. "She's pregnancy." The glass he's holding in his hand falls to the counter. The loud thud echoes through the room. A few other employees turn to see what the commotion is.

"I'm sorry," he says, righting the glass. "I thought you said this girl was pregnant." I just stare at him, never breaking eye contact. "Which would mean that you," He gestures to me. "Are the father." I nod, watching as the information I've just said sinks in. "Holy shit, dude."

"I know." I say, leaning against the bar. "I know."

"How the hell did this happen?" he asks.

"Well, it's like a flower..."I trail off, Tony shoves my chest causing me to laugh.

"Be fucking serious." he sighs at my antics. I should break out into song, but that would be really fucking weird. Besides, the only song that comes to mind is from Grease 2, where the guys sing about reproduction. This is not the time for a musical.

"Anyways," I pick up the next glass, turning back to my work. "She fainted yesterday, and I had to run her to the hospital."

"Damn, bro. Is she okay?" he asks, when I glance over he seems genuinely concerned for someone that he's never even met, and that's how I know he's more than just an employee to me. Because whatever has been thrown at me, I know he will be there to back me up. All the way.

"Yeah, she's good." I place the glass on the shelf under the bar. "It was a scary situation for sure."

"So, are you freaking over being a dad?" he asks, never missing a beat.

"Not really. I mean, I have my moments." I shrug my shoulders. I don't think it's truly hit me full force yet that I'm about to be a father. That a little tiny human will depend so much on me. "It's crazy though, man."

"I'm sure it is." he says. Tossing his rang over his shoulder, he crosses his arms and leans a hip against the counter to face me. "You know I'm always here for you brow, always." I smile.

"Thanks, man. I appreciate it." He nods. I turn, taking a step away from him. "Oh, next time she comes in here asking to speak to me, make sure to tell me about it." I laugh. His face falls.

"Oh, shit." His eyes are wide when he realizes what has happened. "That was her?" I nod. "Fuck, I didn't know."

"It's cool." I smile. "Don't stress it."

"Go be with her, get to know each other. I have everything here covered." I think about what he's said. Tessa was asleep when I left this morning, I didn't want to wake her. She was actually resting. But, I would like to head back to her place and figure out what our plans are going to be. I smile at Tony. "Go." He nudges my shoulder and I don't have to be told twice.

Thankfully, the drive to her house is short and I'm there within a few minutes. When I get to her door, I start to panic but remember that she mentioned having a spare key under the mat. I make a mental note to talk to her about this. It's unsafe, and anyone would think to check there first. I slowly open the door, trying not to make any sounds in case she is still asleep.

When I enter, it's silent. I look around the room, trying to think of what my plan was when I came back. The couch is still a mess from where I left it this morning, douche move. My mom would kick my ass. I walk over, grabbing the blanket and begin folding it neatly.

Afterwards, my stomach growls. I head for the the kitchen, I doubt she's used to having anyone do anything for her, so breakfast is the least I can do.

I find bacon and eggs in the fridge and quickly start getting everything ready. It takes me nearly five minutes to figure out where she keeps all of her utensils and pans. I crack open a few eggs, then get busy missing the ingredients for pancakes based on the measurements on the box. When I rip the bag open, flour goes everywhere. Covering my entire shirt and half of her kitchen. I pull my shirt over my head, tossing it to the floor.

That's how Tessa finds me, half naked cooking her breakfast.

## 22

## TESSA

I WAKE to the smell of bacon and my stomach growls. I begin to panic before I remember that Kyle stayed the night and slept on the couch. Thankfully, today my morning sickness hasn't kicked in. I'm jealous of those women who aren't sick throughout their entire pregnancy, it makes me want to be a lucky one.

I get out of bed; well I roll off the side. That's a more accurate description of that disaster. I'm actually well rested for once; I normally can't get much sleep because of acid reflux. It's a bitch and has been the entire pregnancy, so this kid better come out with a head full of hair or I'll be pissed.

I slide my robe on and tie it in the front, walking down the hallway to the kitchen where Kyle is standing in just his jeans. I study the tattoos across his back, they cover the top half and run just under his hairline. I take in the site of the muscles on his back and how they flex whenever he makes simple movements.

I could get used to waking up to a man like this in my

kitchen making me breakfast. I shake my head, that won't ever happen, Tessa. I have to keep reminding myself of this.

"Good morning." His deep voice startles me, and a small yelp comes out. He chuckles and places a few pieces of bacon on a plate with a scoop of eggs. "Sorry, I didn't mean to scare you."

"That's ok." I flush with embarrassment knowing that I just got caught openly checking him out.

"So, I have a few things to discuss with you." He moves our plates to my small dining room table as I follow. Two glasses of orange juice are already laid out, sitting beside my prenatal vitamins.

"Good things, I hope." I smile as I pop the top to the bottle and swallow one of the large pills. I place the glass to my lips and take a large drink of the orange juice. Kyle watches my every move and his eyes are fixated on my throat.

"Yeah." He clears his throat, and I hide my smile. "First," He pauses, sliding my spare key across the table to me. "This isn't safe." I nod, knowing he is right and there no room for argument. I just keep forgetting to move it somewhere else. "Second, my sister said you have a lamaze class coming up?" he asks, and I nod as I dig into my bacon.

Pregnant girl probs and priorities, man.

"I'd like to come with you, if that's ok with you." He smiles and my heart flutters that he really wants to be a part of this all with me. "I mean, if you'd rather do this by yourself then I understa–"

"Absolutely. This is your child, too," I cut him off. Anything he wants to be a part of, I won't stop him. It would just punish my child in the long run and I refuse to be that woman.

"I know, I just don't want to push you too much." I shake my head; my mouth is full of food, and I'm sure he's probably wondering what the hell he just got into. Tears threaten to form at his words. In all of this, he's currently worried about pushing me too much.

"It's scheduled for Wednesday of this week at four in the afternoon," I say, and watch as he takes out his phone and opens his calendar to enter the date and time.

"Great, I can pick you up." I smile at him in return.

"I'd appreciate that. Thanks." I take another bite of my food and chew it quickly. "So, what was the other thing?" I ask, taking a drink of my orange juice.

"Well, I hope this isn't too fast, but my mom would like to throw you a baby shower," he says, and before I can respond he rushes to finish. "I mean, if you want her, too. You don't have to feel obligated. I think she is just excited but doesn't want to overstep her boundaries." He's rambling now and it's cute.

"Kyle. Stop." I place my hand over his and it shuts him up. He glances down at our joined hands then back up to my eyes. "I think it's a great idea. I was kind of sad that I wasn't going to have one. I've been trying to buy things here and there for the baby, but it all adds up. Plus, I don't know many people here, only a friend I met at the real estate firm."

I can see guilt spread across his face and I feel awful for adding that last part. It wasn't meant to make him feel bad.

"I'm sorry I haven't been here, Tessa."

"Kyle, it's not your fault. You didn't know and I couldn't get ahold of you."

"I'll be here from now on though, you can count on that."

"I know I can." I smile at him as he squeezes my hand gently. Being around him is going to be more difficult than I expected. I'm still attracted to him and my hormones make me a horny heifer.

"Also," he says. I look at him with curiosity. "My parent's neighborhood does this type of annual block party. My parents always host a big dinner in their backyard, and she wants me to bring you."

I think about what he's asking, a block party seems fun, and I'll have to meet his family eventually anyways considering they're the only grandparents that my child will have.

"Sure." He looks shocked.

"Really? I thought I'd have to convince you more." I laugh, shaking my head.

"I'll have to meet them eventually, might as well be now." He nods his head, agreeing with what I'm saying.

Suddenly, I catch myself wondering what his family will think about me and how he will introduce me to everyone.

# 23

# TESSA

KYLE PULLS UP outside my apartment building on Wednesday, thirty minutes early. He's dressed in those jeans I love and a black t-shirt that hugs the muscles on his arms just right. His hair is styled in that messy look and I have to fight the urge to reach out and grab it when he steps in front of me. My mind wanders to the night we had together, and how it felt between my fingers and I have to literally force myself to think of *anything* else to keep from attacking him. His eyes roam down my body and it causes me to clench my legs together to dull the ache. Between his hair and those eyes, I'm a damn lost cause.

"You look gorgeous," he says, as he steps up onto the curb and he kisses my cheek. His simple action causes me to blush. I'm wearing a pair of leggings, because that's really all that is comfortable these days and it looks slightly better than sweatpants. I paired them with an oversized tunic with a fun floral print on it.

He holds the door open to his large truck and I attempt to climb in, failing miserably. My foot slips off the railing and I slide backwards, Kyle's arms reach out to steady me and the contact of his skin on mine send's jolts of electricity through my body. I'm aware of how close he is to my backside, his hands loosen, and he takes a deep breath and slides them down my arms to my hips. With a steady push he helps me into the truck. Once I'm securely buckled, Kyle shuts my door before rounding the truck and jumping into the front seat.

"Where too?" he asks, as he pulls off the curb into traffic.

"It's not far from here," I say, as I pull the map up on my phone and hand it to him. He plugs it into his radio so that it'll display where to go on the screen. His truck looks new, soft leather seats with all black interior. It even has the "new car" scent.

Once we arrive, Kyle takes forever to find parking close to the front door, insisting I don't have to walk very far.

I try to assure him I'm pregnant, not crippled, but he won't hear any of it. He helps me out of the truck and I'm thankful he does after my last mishap. No one wants to see a large pregnant chick rolling across the parking lot. Although, it'd probably be hilarious to see Kyle chasing after me.

When we enter, there are several couples already paired off into their designated spots throughout the room.

"Hello," the instructor says, as she comes to greet us. "Are you scheduled for the class?"

"Yes, Tessa Brooks and this is Kyle," I say, glancing behind me to Kyle. He shakes the instructor's hand and we follow her to an open space.

"Here you go." She hands me a yoga mat. "The class

will begin shortly." She makes her way to the front of the room. Kyle and I find an open spot to set up.

"Welcome, everyone," the instructor begins. I roll the yoga mat out and take a seat at the front and cross my legs. Kyle follows suit and sits directly behind me, mimicking the other dads in the room. His legs are on either side of mine and I try to refocus my attention back to the front of the room, but I struggle when he places his arms atop his knees and his thumb grazes against the side of my arm. Little chill bumps appear and I shiver slightly from the touch. Being this close to him is still an adjustment.

Kyle's hand runs up and down my arm and I feel him lean in. His chest is against my back and I can feel his breath close to my ear.

"You cold?" he whispers. I'm unable to form a coherent sentence so I just nod.

"We have a good-sized class this go around and I am so excited that you all will be welcoming sweet little babies into the world soon." She smiles and glances around the room. "The goal of lamaze is to build a mother's confidence in her ability to give birth." She looks around the room. "We will do this throughout all of the classes and it will help pregnant women understand how to cope with the pain associated with birth that will facilitate labor and promote comfort," she continues discussing the importance of the class, and I allow my eyes to roam the other couples in the room.

I'm by far the youngest here, many look like they're in their late twenties and early thirties. I lean against Kyle who pushes his head forward so that his ear is close to my mouth.

"How old are you?" He turns his head so that he can see my eyes and his brows crease.

"What?" he asks, obviously confused by where this question came from.

"How old are you?" I whisper again.

"Twenty-nine," he says, and I turn my attention back to the class. He's obviously the right age of our peers. "How old are you?" His lips brush against my ear accidentally and I jump at the contact.

"Twenty-one." His brows rise in surprise. "How old did you think I was?"

"Hell, I don't know. You just seem older than that." I shrug and look back at the instructor. Fear clouds my mind. Will my age become an issue?

"How much will labor hurt? That's a question everyone wants the answer to and truthfully, I can't give you an exact rate. Some women can handle pain without any medication while others will be attempting to turn their dosage up on the IV machine." The class chuckles at her joke. I can one-hundred percent assure everyone I will be the one cranking that shit up. I hate pain and I cannot handle it for long periods of time.

For the next hour, we discuss breathing techniques and ways our significant others can help reduce some of the nerves and pain during labor. By the time our short recess comes around, I'm feeling much more confident than when I walked in.

Along the back wall is a small table with an assortment of snacks and drinks. Kyle and I both wander over to get us something. *Momma's gotta eat.*

"Hello." A woman in line ahead of me stops. "You two

are just the cutest things and you are adorable pregnant."
She eyes my bump as I take a few cookies on a napkin.

"Thank you," I say, sweetly.

"How far along are you?"

"Thirty-two weeks," I say, and my hand instinctively
rubs my belly. It's something I've noticed I've been doing
more and more recently. Kyle nudges me along as a line is
growing behind him, so I step out of the way with the lady
while he continues. "You?" I point towards her very large
belly.

"Thirty-six weeks, tomorrow." She smiles down at her
bump as her spouse steps beside her. "This one has went
fast."

"How many kids do you have?" I ask.

"This is our third. I'm at the stage now where I don't
give a damn how bad it hurts, I'm just ready to feel
comfortable again," she giggles, and I can't help but
join in.

"I understand. I miss sleeping on my stomach." I sigh.
I've never been a back sleeper so being pregnant has been a
struggle. I can sleep on my side most nights, but it's not
the same. I miss being able to throw my leg up and be
completely on my stomach with my hands buried underneath my pillow.

"Here ya go," Kyle says, as he steps beside me. He
hands me a small cup with what looks like lemonade in it.

"Thank you." I smile up at him.

"You two." She pauses and smiles at her husband. "You
may be the cutest couple we have seen in a while. Reminds
me of the two of us in the beginning."

"Oh, no. It's not what you think," I correct. Her brows

pinch together in confusion. "We aren't a couple," I say awkwardly, looking to Kyle for help.

"Oh, I'm sorry. I just assumed." She blushes. "Really, I'm sorry. Excuse us." She turns and heads towards their spot on the floor. I watch as the two of them move, and the way her husband helps guide her to the floor is sweet. I long for that type of interaction, wondering if Kyle will be that for me someday.

"Well, that was awkward," Kyle says, when I turn to face him. I facepalm myself which causes him to laugh. "You should have just gone along with it."

I wonder about his comment for the rest of the class. Was he serious or was it something he just said?

After we finish our snacks, class resumes. The couple we spoke with earlier avoids all eye contact with us, making Kyle and I laugh.

## 24

## KYLE

LAMAZE CLASS WASN'T AS bad as I expected. Tessa intently listened for most of the class. But I noticed every time I touched her, she'd hold her breath and wouldn't release it until my hands moved. It's nice to know my touch has the same effect on her as her touch does me.

The look on her face when the couple had mistaken us for a couple was hilarious. When she turned to me for support, I totally let her suffer that one out on her own. It really wouldn't be so bad to be in a relationship, if I got to wake up to her every morning.

*Whoa. What the fuck? Where did that come from?*

I don't date. At all. I'm the king of one-night stands. Maybe two, if I think the girl is worth it. Granted, all of that will change now that I'll have a baby. I doubt the baby stays with me much until he is a little older, but still, times are changing for me.

I've never had a girlfriend, in all of my twenty-nine years of life. Not even in elementary school. I like variety. That may make me sound awful, but every girl typically knows what they are getting into. It's an agreement I make sure I'm usually clear on. Except for Tessa, she made it clear with me that it was only *one* night.

Something about waking up to the other side of the bed being empty when Tessa snuck out the next morning didn't settle right. I had plans for one more round, but she was long gone by the time my eyes opened, and I was pissed about it.

I haven't seen Tessa in about a week. I've tried to give her some space to adjust to having me in the picture. I've texted her nearly every day though to check on her and we chat on the phone at night.

The block party is tonight and my parents are thrilled that Tessa has agreed to come with me. When I arrive outside her apartment, I walk as quickly as I can to her door. When she opens it, she's wearing denim shorts that are frayed at the bottom, and a tank top that has two tiny feet printed over her pregnant belly. She's fucking cute.

"You ready?" I ask, she steps out into the sun and squints.

"Let me get my sunglasses." I wait as she rushes abc in and grabs them. She shuts the door behind her and starts walking towards my truck. I take the opportunity to check out the curves she's gained from the pregnancy.

*And what good curves they are.*

I open the door and help her climb in. Once she is situated, I shut the door and climb into the driver's side.

"So, tell me. What are your parents like?" she asks. I think about her questions, trying to find the best way to describe my family.

"Well, my mom will want to hug you as soon as she sees you, so be ready for that." I turn to look at her. "My dad, well he's great. He's the best man I know. My sister and I were blessed with our parents."

"That sounds wonderful." she says, and I'm about to ask her about her parents but I pull into my parent's neighborhood. The road is blocked so we have a little walk to get to their house.

"Tell me if you get too hot, okay?" I ask, concerned about her being in the heat for too long.

"Kyle, I'll be fine." She assures me, but I still worry. Walking up the sidewalk, I watch Tessa as she stares at all the houses. It's a rich neighborhood, but everyone who lives here would give the shirt off their back for anyone. They're all good people. "What does everyone know about me?" she asks, I shrug my shoulders because I'm honestly not sure what anyone knows.

"I guess we will find out shortly." I point to where my mom is all but running towards the two of us. She's dressed in white shorts and a denim top.

"Oh, hi." she says as she approaches. "You must be Tessa?" She pulls her in for a hug and I catch the look Tessa shoots me before she does. I tried to warn her. "My God, you're glowing." I watch a blush creep up her neck, and it's fucking sexy.

"My boy." My mother says to me next, she pulls me down to her level and I squeeze her like I always do, finishing it with a peck to the cheek.

"Hi, mom."

"So, Tessa." My mom turns her attention back to Tessa, grabbing her hand and begins pulling her away from me. I follow, because I don't have much of a choice right now. "You're absolutely gorgeous."

"Thank you." Tessa says in her shy voice. "Thank you for having me today."

"Oh, nonsense. You're family now." I can visibly see Tessa relax her shoulders and it makes me feel good knowing that she's becoming more comfortable.

"That's sweet. So, tell me about this block party. I've never been to one." That sends my mom on a long spiel about how the block party was started and what everyone is responsible for. My dad approaches, handing me a beer.

"Hey." I say, popping the top of the bottle, clinking it against his.

"Your mother is smitten." He points his bottle to where my mom is standing with Tessa.

"I'll say so." Just then, I'm smacking in the back of the head.

"Well, if it isn't my brother." My sister steps up beside me, throwing her arm over my shoulder. "Glad you came."

"Ha." I've skipped the last few block parties. It really isn't my scene.

"I'm going to go say hi to Tessa." My sister leaves the two of us standing, staring at the three of them. The smile Tessa gives my sister lets me know that she feels comfortable around her, and it puts me at ease.

I'm enjoying my self until I see Tim Schaeder approach them. I went to school with him, he's a preppy asshole that acts like he's entitled to any and everything he wants. My sister doesn't give him the time of day, so he turns his attention to Tessa.

*Fuck no. She's mine.*

Moving my attention to where they're standing, I watch as he holds his hand out for her. Tessa is polite, shaking his hand and turning her attention back to what my sister is saying. That's when his hand reaches the small of her back, and I lose all my restraint.

Moving around the crowd, I come up behind Tessa. Placing my hands on her hips, I move her to the other side so that she is away from Tim. Tim's expression changes as he watches the exchange.

"Well, Kyle. I didn't expect to see you here, it's been a while." He holds his hand out to me.

"Tim." I attempt to turn my attention back to Tessa and my sister, but he speaks again.

"How have you been, man?" he asks.I drop my hand from Tessa's hip and turn to him. My sister cuts me a look that tells me to chill out, so I do. Tim was a dickhead back in high school, and we never got along. He spread some shit about my sister, and I wasn't too keen on the idea of letting him get away with it. So, I beat the shit out of him. Twice.

"I've been good." I say, and I have.

""Ah, still running that little bar of yours?" And there's the dig. *That little bar of yours.*

"Yeah, that *little bar* is kicking ass." Stress my words so he gets the point. I'm not sure if she can sense that I'm getting pissed off, but Tessa's hand finds mind. Her hands slowly slides into mine, with her fingers intertwining and holding tightly. The movement catches Tim's attention and he glances down to our joined hands. His brows shoot up in curiosity.

"Do you two know each other?" he asks. Which is a stupid question, considering she's standing here, holding my hand. Not to mention her swollen stomach.

I nod, not giving him a verbal response to his stupid ass

question. My sister has walked off, so I pull Tessa with me. "Excuse us."

"What was that about?" Tessa asks once we're out of earshot of Tim.

"Long story." I gesture to a table set up in my parents backyard, it's loaded with different finger foods. Grabbing both of us a plate, I grab what she points at. Once we sit, I start to explain. "So, when we were in high school, my sister went out with Tim. At the end of the date, he attempted to kiss her, but she refused. She said the date wasn't what she had hoped it would be and didn't want to kiss him." I take a bite of a jalapeño popper. "Tim tried to force her into kissing him, and after my sister lost it on him, he finally kicked her out of the car and left."

"Wow." Tessa says. "What a dick." She looks over her shoulder in the direction of Tim.

"Agreeing with her, I nod my head and finish my popper. "The next day at school, he begins spreading lies about my sister. Talking about how easy she was, what a terrible lay she is, all the ruthless shit a teenage boy that was rejected says. So, basically I just beat his ass."

"Your poor sister." She reaches her hand over the table to mine. "You two seem close."

"We are." I glance to where my sister is standing with my mom and a few of her friends. "We always have been. And rarely fight, she just has piss poor taste in men. Tim isn't even the tip of that iceberg."

"That's sweet."

"What about you?" I ask. "Any siblings?"

She shakes her head, "No, I was an only child. As far as I know." That last part piques my curiosity but I don't ask her any more on the topic. A block party isn't the place for this conversation.

"Want a drink?" I ask, pushing away from the table we're sitting at.

"Please."

## 25

## TESSA

Watching Kyle walk away, I don't even notice his mother and sister sit down beside me until his mother clears her throat. When I turn to look at the two of them, they're wearing a knowing smile that causes me to blush because I was just caught checking him out.

"So, tell me, dear." His mother begins. She's a sweet lady, blonde hair to her shoulders, without a single hair out of place. "Tell me more about yourself." I flinch because I don't like talking about myself, at all. It's awkward and there really isn't that much to tell.

"I'm a realtor. I just moved here about nine months ago, I needed a change and this is where I landed." I say, honestly. I'm silently begging her not to ask me about my family, I really hate talking about them, it brings up old wounds and it's like pouring salt into them.

"That's wonderful. Do you enjoy your job?" she asks. I look at her face, only curiosity is found.

"I do. I wasn't sure I would when I began, but it has really become a passion for me." I grab a chip from my plate and break it in half. "Plus, it'll be easy for me when the baby comes to work from home." She nods, understanding.

"Well, anytime you need to go into the office, you call grandma and I'll come running for that sweet baby." I smile, a genuine smile because I know she means every word she is saying.

"I will probably hit you up on that." I say, laughing. His family is so easy going, and they put me at ease for the unknown future. Kyle and I have no idea what our lives hold, other than being tied together for the rest of our lives because of this sweet baby boy.

"What are you ladies talking about?" He returns, sitting a red solo cup of sweet tea in front of me. I pick the cup up, placing it to my lips and taste the sugary goodness. Ah, sweet tea.

"Oh, just baby talk." his mother says. His sister has been quiet, when I look over at her, she's watching me. I furrow my brows but she just smiles at me.

"I'm about to head out." Lou says, she pushes away from the table and wraps her arms around her mother's shoulder, kissing her on the cheek. She moves to Kyle who embraces her in a full hug, and I'm slightly jealous because I want his arms around me.

Next she turns to me, gesturing for me to hug her. I stand, as quickly as I can with this belly, and she engulfs me in a hug that is only meant for family members, and I feel at peace in this moment. Accepted by a family that doesn't have to take me in, but is obviously willing to. My arms wrap around his sister, and I fight the tears that are threatening to come. Kyle must sense my emotion, because he moves closer to me and when she releases me, his arm is firmly across my back offering the support I desperately need.

"Y'all have fun." Lou says and heads towards the row of cars lined on both sides of the street. Kyle's father walks over, taking the seat next to his mother.

"So, have we decided names for this little guy yet?" He asks, Kyle and I both sit back down.

"No. We haven't really talked about it much." Kyle looks at me.

"I figure once we see him, we will just know." I shrug my shoulders.

"That's a fun one." His dad the typical dad. Denim shorts, a t-shirt with an apron on that says 'Grill Master', and a white pair of New Balance tennis shoes. The American Father. "You two go on and walk down the block. I know there are lots of fun foods out there." Kyle stands, offering me his hand. I take it, and I'm kind of excited to see what these annual parties are all about.

Thankfully, his parents' neighborhood is mostly shaded, so the tree covering offers a cool atmosphere. If I were standing in the sun all day, I'd probably pass out from heat exhaustion.

As we're walking, I see several kids playing hopscotch in the road. I smile, thinking of my child soon being out there, enjoying this festivity. Their laughter is all you can hear.

"That'll be our boy someday." Kyle says in my ear, the chill bumps of him being so near return. I turn to him, and he's smiling down at me.

"I can't wait."

"Me either." We walk a little further and I notice face paint- ing, and then I zero in on the cotton candy machine and the baby must want some because he begins going crazy. Placing my hand on my stomach, I let out a small gasp, causing Kyle's face to morph into worry.

"You okay?" I smile at him, grabbing his hand and placing it on the spot where he just kicked. We wait for a moment before Kyle finally feels him, and the smile on his face could drop me to my damn knees. I hope like hell our son gets his father's smile, because it truly does light up a room.

"Cotton candy?" he asks after the kicking has calmed down.

"You don't even have to ask." I say, marching towards the stand. When I get closer, a stick of cotton candy is handed to me and I rejoin Kyle. "You didn't want any?" I ask, confused on why he didn't get any.

"Nah, I'm fine. I'm not big on sweets." I pause, looking up at him with disgust on my face.

"How in the hell do you not like sweets?" I ask. "That's so unnatural of you." He laughs, but my face doesn't falter.

"I don't know, I've just never really liked it. I can eat it, I just prefer not to." I pinch a piece of the cotton candy off, sticking it to his lips. He's confused by my action, and to be honest I have no idea what the hell I'm doing, but I hold the cotton candy there anyways. He stares down at me, then without any emotion, he grabs my wrist. Opening his mouth, his tongue darts out and the cotton candy begins to melt against it. I watch as he slowly closes his mouth, covering my fingertips and it immediately sets me on fucking fire. Once I come to my senses, I remember that we are in the middle of a block party in his parents neighborhood, surrounded by little kids in front of a cotton candy booth. This is not the time or the place to jump him.

He laughs, but takes my fingers and kisses them. We begin walking again, reaching a karaoke section. I nudge him. "Go on, sing something." Expecting him to laugh it off, he turns, winks at me and disappears through the crowd.

I stand in the crowd, enjoying my cotton candy. Once I'm finished I find the nearest trash can, discarding the stick.

"Next up, Kyle Tucker." My eyes widen, he steps onto the makeshift stage in his jeans and black t-shirt. The music begins and I immediately recognize the words.

*Just the Way by Parmalee.*

He sings every word, and I'm shocked at how good he is. If he did this at the bar, he'd have a full house every night. He sings the words, but his eyes never leave mine. My hips sway to the beat of the song, and his words seem to be more than just the song. When the song ends, he points directly at me, causing the crowd to part and look.

My blush creeps up my neck at the attention he has just directed on me. I smile awkwardly, and listen as everyone around me says things like, "How sweet." or "Gosh, that was precious."

Kyle finally rejoins me, and I swat at his stomach, which causes him to laugh and pull me against him. Our noses are touching, we're so close and I know everyone around us is watching too. I expect his head to dip, but he surprises me when he places a soft kiss against the tip of my nose and releases me. Threading his fingers through mine.

We begin walking back towards the entrance of the party, stopping to tell his parents bye.

"CALL us if you need anything at all, dear." His mother says. His father shakes Kyle's hand, and we walk hand in hand back to his truck.

Once inside, he turns the truck on and I'm thankful for the cool air blowing against my skin.

"What'd you think?" He asks, turning his truck around and exiting their neighborhood.

"It was fun." I say, "I really enjoyed it. Everyone seems so close knit.

"They are. It's been that way my entire life, it's a great place to live." He adds. "One day, I'd like to live there." And my mind immediately returns to what it would be like if the three of us were a family, enjoying block parties and all of the fun gatherings the neighborhood has.

# 26

# KYLE

IT'S BEEN a few weeks since the block party and my mom managed to throw together a baby shower for Tessa in a short amount of time. Tessa has been so excited about it all. It's being held at my parents' house, so I offered to drive Tessa.

Just as I expected, she is opening the door as I walk up. She's wearing a royal blue dress that flows at the bottom but is tight around her baby bump. I have to adjust my jeans to situate myself at the sight of her, because she is fucking gorgeous.

Her hair is loose and curled at the ends, she has on minimal makeup, but it's perfect for her.

*She looks perfect.*

I round the truck to open her door and help her in. My truck is so big, that she always struggles climbing in. My hands automatically go to her hips as she climbs in, this time with ease. I pat the side of her thigh as she buckles before I shut her door and move to the driver's side.

"You excited?" I ask as I climb in. I buckle myself up

and check my mirrors before pulling away from the curb. It's about a 20-minute drive to my parents' house, and it's filled with a comfortable silence. We listen to the radio, and Tessa hums along to the tune of whatever song is on. It's nice.

When we pull up to my parents' driveway, I watch Tessa's expression as she takes in the house again, when she saw it before it was covered in decorations for the block party. Lou and I grew up well taken care of, but we were always taught to work hard for what we wanted. This is why our parents supported us in any career choice we wanted, and Lou paid her own way through med school, which was hard as hell, but I think she benefited from it in the long run.

"Holy shit, Kyle. It's more beautiful than I remember." I watch her face light up when she sees the home. It's an old colonial style home with large pillars lining the front porch. The driveway is a long gravel that circles in front of the house. My parents have decorated the outside with a ton of blue balloons and even created a balloon archway above the front door.

"Yeah, but don't get any ideas. I wasn't raised as a rich boy." I chuckle.

I park closest to the front door, so Tessa doesn't have to walk as far. I help her out of the truck and take her hand to lead her to the front door. When we step through, we are immediately greeted by my parents, and her hand tightens in mine. My mom gushes over Tessa to all of her friends, and I'm enjoying watching the blush creep up the side of her neck.

I lean into Tessa's ear, it catches her off guard, and she jumps, so my hands hold her firmly in place.

"That blush looks sexy as hell," I say before pulling away. She turns her head slightly to look up at me, and I swear the blush gets darker in color.

"Son." I turn to my father's voice. "Let's go out back and have a beer." I nod but turn my attention back to Tessa.

"Will you be okay by yourself for a bit?" I ask. I won't leave her if she's uncomfortable. I know my mom will take good care of her and the two of them hit it off at the block party, but there are some women here I'd rather she didn't have a run-in with. Viv being one. I'm not sure why Lou even invited her.

"Sure. I'm fine. Go have fun." She smiles and moves to where my mom stands with a group of women. She fits in well here and something in my chest aches.

I follow dad through the house and out the back door. They have a large deck attached to the back of the house that overlooks a large pond. It's nice, especially in the evening time.

I sit in one of the large wooden chairs as my dad pops the top of a beer and hands it to me. I place the bottle against my lips and taste the cool liquid.

"So, how are you holding up?" I turn to look at him.

"I'm doing good," I reply honestly. "Staying busy between the bar and Tessa." "Your sister said you attended a Lamaze class with her?" I laugh and nod. "I'm proud of you, son." That catches my atten- tion. I look at him, and his face is nothing but a smile. "You've really stepped into this role, and you could have easily walked away. I know this wasn't the way you planned to have kids, but I'm still really proud of you, boy."

"Thanks, dad." I swallow the lump in my throat. We

aren't typically the father and son that share feelings like this, so it's difficult for both of us. I hear a round of cheers come from inside the house. "I better go see what all that fuss is."

We both stand together, and he clasps my shoulder and gives me a bear hug. The only hugs dad knows how to give. My poor mother has complained about them my entire life, but she always smiles whenever he wraps his arms around her and gives her one.

When I enter the living room, my eyes immediately find the mother of my child. She's sitting in a chair closest to the fire- place, and my sister sits beside her with a pen and notebook. Tessa grabs the next present and opens the card.

"This is from Kyle's parents." she says as she hands the card to Lou, who then places it in the small stack of cards beside her. Tessa reaches into the tissue filled bag and pulls out several outfits, all in baby blue and gray. There is a pack of bottles, several pacifiers, and a piece of paper. When she opens it, I can see her eyes fill with tears. Without even thinking, I'm making my way across the room towards her. I squat beside her and place my hand on her knees.

"Baby? What is it?" She looks at me, and the tears nearly fall. "Look." She hands me the paper she's been looking at, and when I take it from her, I see it's the crib she has been wanting but couldn't justify spending that much money on. I smile up at her and place a soft kiss on her cheek before turning my attention to my mother.

She stands near the back of the room, a hand against her heart as my dad wraps his arms around her. I make my way over to her and wrap her in my arms and thank her. Her tears fall as Tessa moves across the room. She moves flawlessly, and her dress flowing behind her makes her look like an angel. Every eye in the room is watching her, she handles pregnancy so well, and I'm a damn lucky man. I move to the side when she approaches so she can thank my parents.

After opening gifts, everyone begins eating the cake my mom and sister had prepared for the evening. I glance up to see Vivian in front of Tessa.

I'm unsure of what is being said until I see Tessa take a step towards Viv, and I know I need to step in before something happens.

## 27

### TESSA

THE BABY SHOWER was going great until *Vivian* decided she needed to speak with me.

"I just want you to know that whatever you think you have going on with Kyle, it'll all be over soon enough." She wears a smile the entire time she says it, and while nothing is going on with Kyle and I, I don't appreciate her choice of time or place to have this conversation. I guess now is as good of a time as any to let her know that.

"That's for Kyle to decide, don't you think?" I smirk at her. My eyes glance to the side and I see Kyle watching us. His arms are crossed, and his legs are spread wide. I'd take the time to look him over, but I'm preoccupied by this dumb bitch. "Also, this isn't the time or place to have this conversation, Vivian. So please, go get a piece of cake and enjoy the rest of the shower." I turn to walk away from her, but she grabs my arm pulling me back towards her.

"Oh, honey, you are naive if you think that having a baby will change that man. He's a player, honey." She steps in close to me, dropping her voice. I glance down at her hand on my arm and become furious. She has no right to put her hands on me. "And up until a few months ago, you were the whore that didn't even know who the father was. Are we even sure he is the father? You don't look like his type."

All I see after that is red. This bitch. I take a step closer to her and make sure she sees me as I get in her face. I'm not normally this confrontational, but she has crossed a line and hit a nerve. Talking about me is one thing, but she just brought my son into the mix. Suddenly, I don't give a damn where we are or what is happening around me because all I see is her.

"Listen here, bitc–" Before I can finish my sentence, Kyle is stepping between us, his back turned to me. His eyes are hard as he stares her down.

"What the fuck, Viv?" he says, his arm is behind him and he's holding my hand. I hadn't even realized I was shaking until he squeezes it gently.

"Kyle," she says, shocked by his sudden appearance. "Tessa and I were just discussing the baby."

"Cut the shit. I heard what you said, and I'll tell you this once and only once. Do not fucking talk about the mother of my child. Do not talk about our child. If you do, I will ruin you and you know I fucking can," he says, and even I flinch from behind him. "This is my family you are talking about and I won't fucking stand around and hear the bullshit flow from your lips."

"Kyle, it's not what you think. I was just looking out for you; she seems like a gold-digger only after your money. Are you even sure the baby is yours?" Her voice grows then, and I slowly turn my head to see everyone in the room has grown silent at our altercation. I tug on Kyle's hand and he glances around the room. His demeanor changes, growing colder. His parents and sister stand a few feet away, watching the altercation and I'm so embarrassed that this has happened. They were being such wonderful hosts and Vivian had to ruin the entire damn thing.

"I told you not to talk about Tessa or our child again." His voice raises to a tone that has Vivian shaking where she stands. "Get the fuck out of this house." he says it in such a nasty voice, that several around the room gasp. Vivian's face is bright red, but I can't tell if it's from embarrassment of being kicked out of the baby shower or anger from having Kyle do it. Either way, I'm not sad to see her stomp across the living room and out the front door. Kyle turns his attention back to me, his chest rising and falling with his deep breaths.

"Are you ok?" he asks, his arms going around each side of me. He bends so he is eye level with me. His eyes bounce back and forth between mine, searching.

"I'm fine. She just makes me so damn mad," he chuckles, before leaning in and placing a sweet kiss against my forehead. When I look around, everyone begins mingling as if nothing happened.

Shortly after, the baby shower is over and everyone says their goodbyes to Kyle and I. I watch as Kyle begins loading up all the gifts in his truck.

"Tessa, are you ok?" Lou comes to stand beside me.

"I'm fine. I'm sorry about that, I'm so embarrassed." I cover my face with my hands. "Oh my gosh, your parents." I look around for them.

"Don't be, Viv has been that way for as long as I can remember. She's had a thing for Kyle since she started working for me three years ago, but honestly I think it's about time I change that." My brows shoot clear up to my hairline. "No one will disrespect the mother of my nephew. *No one.*" She winks at me and gives me a small hug. "I'll see you this week, right?"

"Yes, on Wednesday. Thanks again for helping throw me a shower," I say, and I truly mean it. Without Kyle's family, our baby wouldn't have anyone.

Lou smiles before moving to kiss her mother and father goodbye. Kyle's parents move towards me then as I'm stacking the last set of diapers for Kyle to grab.

"Tessa, I hope this shower was everything you wanted." She smiles.

"Yes, minus the little Vivian episode." Kyle's father rolls his eyes. "I'm just glad someone finally put her in her place." I'm relieved hearing how everyone feels about her, and that they don't appear to be upset with my outburst.

"Thank you for hosting this for me, I was really sad at the thought of not having a shower," I say. "And thank you so much for the crib. I absolutely love it."

"It's being delivered to your apartment tomorrow morning; will you be home?" she asks. Monday's are my easy days, so I normally don't even make it into the office.

"Yes."

"Great, I'll make sure Kyle is there to help." She moves towards the door where Kyle is entering.

"We are really excited to be grandparents, Tessa." Kyle's father places an arm around my shoulder and squeezes gently. I smile up at him and can't help but feel grateful at the turn of events in my life.

# 28

# KYLE

WHEN WE GET BACK to Tessa's house, I get to work unloading the back of my truck. We have so many diapers, but she assured me that these would only last a few months. I'm not sure how a kid can shit that much, but I figure she's more of an expert than me.

When I bring the last load up, she's sitting cross legged on the living room floor. There are empty gift bags and tissue paper everywhere.

"Whoa." That's a lot of clothes. I gesture to the large pile beside her. She continues pulling pieces out of the current bag she is digging through and adding them to the top.

"I know. He's going to be so cute in it all." I sit the bags in my hand down near her and move to sit on the couch closest to where she is sitting. She looks so happy going through all the bags and organizing everything, I could sit here and watch her all day.

Eventually, we start moving things to the baby's room.

She had it painted a soft baby blue color and the dresser is a light gray against one wall.

"Where will you be putting the crib? Mom said it would be delivered tomorrow morning?" I turn to survey the rest of the room.

"I'm thinking along this big wall here," she says, as she moves across the room to stand in the spot, she wants the crib.

We get to work organizing the clothing by size and stacking the boxes of diapers at the bottom of the closet. His closet is already packed full, I'm not sure he could receive much more at this point.

I work on getting the stroller and car seat put together, while she throws the trash away and unpacks all the lotions and soaps. Once we are finished, we both stand in the doorway looking at our son's room. Tessa moves to hold her back.

"You ok?" I ask, concern is present in my voice.

"Yeah, I'm fine. I'm just tired after this long day." She smiles as she massages the lower part of her back, the best she can.

"Why don't you go take a warm bath?" I say. I know she isn't supposed to submerge herself into hot water, so a warm one will be soothing for her.

"Yeah?"

"Yeah, I'll go make us something to eat. You've had a long day, go relax." Without thinking, I lean over and press a kiss against her temple before striding down the hallway to her kitchen.

I find the ingredients for stir fry in the fridge, so I get to work on making it. After I'm finished, I throw some of the food onto plates and pour us both a glass of sweet tea.

It's been about forty-five minutes, so I move to the bathroom.

I can hear some soft music playing and the smell of lavender is strong. I knock on the door, but get no response.

"Tessa?" I say, as I knock again. Still no response.

I press the door open and slowly peak in. Tessa has her head leaned against the back of the tub and looks peacefully relaxed. She turns her head slowly to look at me.

"Hey, food's ready. You almost done?" I ask, as I step through the door and grab the towel hanging on the rack I'm stopped in my tracks. Seeing her in the tub, completely exposed with the water resting just below her pink nipples. Her stomach sits just slightly above the water, and her long legs are arched and resting on the other side of the tub.

I take a step closer to the tub, her eyes follow my every move. My breathing has picked up and I can see the rapid rise and fall of her chest. I grab the sponge that is resting on the edge of the tub and gently place it in the water, soaping it up then I begin to wash her body with it.

At the touch of the sponge on her skin, she arches her back and a soft moan slips past her full lips. I fight the urge to lean down and take her lips with mine. I continue running the sponge along each breast and down over her stomach. When I get close to the spot between her legs, I dip the sponge in the water and then bring it up above her legs, and squeeze the excess water so it drips down her leg. When the sponge touches her again, she gasps and her lips part, making me horny as hell.

"Please, Kyle." Her voice is so low, almost a murmur. "Please touch me."

I drop the sponge to the water and let my hand fall to

her knee. Her skin is so soft from the lavender water as I run my hand down to her thigh. I move to her inner thigh and move my eyes to hers. She's watching me, her chest rising and falling. I run my hand up her center, but don't stop as I move to her breasts. I take one in my hand and pinch her taut nipple; her head falls back against the tub and she shifts her body.

My hand moves lower, trailing over her stomach. Looking at her, pregnant with my child is one of the sexiest things I have ever seen. I dip my hand into the water and stroke between her wet lips. Her eyes close at my touch. I begin stroking her hard clit, her soft moans cause me to bite my lips. Seeing her like this is damn near enough to make me go in my jeans like I'm in junior high again. I move my fingers lower, and push one into her tight, wet pussy. I bite my lip harder at the feel of her pussy tightening around my finger. I add a second, working them together. In and out and rub her clit with my thumb. I can feel the beginning of her orgasm, so I work my fingers harder and faster, curling them to hit the spot I know she likes so much.

"Come for me, baby," I say, and she tightens at my words. "Come all over my fingers." I curl my fingers again and press down hard on her clit. She tightens around my fingers; her head rises to make eye contact with me, but falls back quickly when I start moving my fingers again. She grips the side of the tub and she cries out my name as she comes undone.

I grab a towel for her as she relaxes and to get her breathing evened out.

"Can you stand right now?" I ask with a cocky smirk, holding the towel open wide for her. She rolls her eyes, but

I don't miss the small hint of a smile playing on her lips. She steps out of the tub and turns her back to me so I can wrap her in the towel.

"Dinner is ready," I say, and hold the door open for her as she exits to her room to get dressed.

## 29

# TESSA

K YLE LEFT last night after dinner, so we didn't get a chance to discuss what happened during my bath. Having his hands on me was nearly too much to handle, and I'm so embarrassed that I begged him to touch me, but I needed it.

*My god. That man's hands.*

It was just like I remembered the last time. The way he hits my spot every single time. I woke up this morning feeling better than I have in months.

There is a knock at my door, so I move to look through the peep hole. Two delivery men stand outside, with a box that I am assuming is the crib. I swing the door wide to allow them entry. Before I shut the door, Kyle is stepping through also.

"Good morning," I say, as he steps inside. He winks as I shut the door behind him. "Right down the hall, this way." I move in front of the delivery men and show them the way to the baby's room. They move the box to the wall that is empty.

Kyle moves in behind us, when I glance at him, he's shooting daggers at one of the men. I look to the guy, but he is obviously oblivious to Kyle's staring and his eyes are trained on my boobs. I look down to realize I only have on my tank top that I slept in and my boobs are nearly spilling out the top. One of the downfalls of my breast growing during pregnancy.

"Well, thank you," I say, trying to avert his attention as I maneuver my straps to cover my boobs better. His eyes linger a moment longer before Kyle steps in front of me. That catches his attention. He nods at Kyle then moves towards the front door.

"If you need any help assembling, please call me." He holds out a card with his phone number visibly printed on the back side. Kyle takes the card from him that was meant for me.

"I think I've got it. Thanks though. There's the front door," Kyle says. I giggle at his bluntness; he's obviously bothered by the guy.

When the door shuts behind them on their way out, Kyle turns his attention to me. His eyes bounce between my eyes and my boobs.

"Well, wasn't that nice of him," I laugh, as he rolls his eyes. He stomps towards the baby's room and I follow, still chuckling at his expense.

"Shut up," he says, as he pulls a pocket knife out, flicking the blade open and cuts the tape on the side of the cardboard box. He pulls several pieces out of the box and lays them around the empty floor.

"Man, that looks like a lot of work. Let me just go find that card and give them a call, I'm sure they'll come back and assemble it for us." I'm still laughing as I attempt to run out of the room, but Kyle wraps his strong arms around my waist and pulls me back against his chest. I collapse and giggle against him. He chuckles in my ear.

"You better watch yourself, momma." Him calling me momma makes me melt. I turn my head to look at him, but we are closer than I expected. Our lips are nearly touching before I break the connection and step away. Forcing him to drop his arms.

"So, what do you think of the crib?" I ask, as I move to where the pieces are scattered around the floor.

"I like the color. I think it'll look great in here," he says, as he moves beside me, scanning the pieces.

We spend the next few hours assembling the crib. We discuss his family and his childhood and what type of father he hopes to be. Someone just like his father.

"What about you?" he asks, as we are adding the finishing touches on the crib. I pull the crib bedding from the corner of the room and start opening the package.

"What do you mean?"

"What about your past? You never talk about it much." My hands freeze on the zipper. Talking about my past isn't something I enjoy speaking of. But I promise to fight like hell to be a better parent than the one I was left with. I had shitty foster homes before I ended up with the Brown's. I was too old to be adopted and they wanted younger children. I'm lucky they allowed me to stay past my eighteenth birthday the way they did.

"Well, I was in foster care." My admission causes him to drop the screwdriver he's using. His eyes look at me and they are full of pity and I hate it. It's one of the reasons I hate discussing my past. I don't need anyone's pity, nothing about it changes what happened. He grabs the screwdriver and turns his full attention on me.

"I had no idea," he says, his tone is gentle. "What happened?"

Where to begin, it's been so long since I've told this story. Most of the time, it was told for me and I just observed the different versions being told. Foster family after foster family.

"My mom died when I was eight. She worked a lot of long hours, so I rarely got much quality time with her, but when she died it was just me and my dad. He was totally different back then. He was a good dad, always involved. When he lost her, he just sort of lost himself." I wipe the stray tear that rolls down my cheek. It's been so long since I've cried over this part of my life. Kyle moves to squat in front of me. He doesn't reach out and I'm thankful, I'm not sure I could contain my emotions if he touched me right now. "She died in a car accident on her way home from the hospital, she was a nurse."

I replay the events of that day in my mind. The sadness on my dad's face when the officers came to our door to tell us the news. I remember him falling to the floor, the officer trying to console him, but he couldn't.

"My dad turned to alcohol shortly after. He wasn't mean or anything, he just checked out." I shrug my shoulders. "He forgot he had a daughter; I began missing school. Food was harder to get ahold of and eventually, one of my teachers noticed and called in the hotline. We had social workers stop in and conduct interviews and he drank right through the entire thing. They took me to my room, had me pack and bag and walked me out the front door. He didn't even look at me as I left." I look at

Kyle; his eyes are sad. "That was the last time I ever saw him."

"I'm sorry, Tess." His hands reach out and take mine in his. He rubs his calloused thumb back and forth over the back of my hand. "I had no idea."

"It's fine. I've made peace with it all," I say, and turn my attention back to the crib bedding. I stand, or well more like roll to my hands and knees and then attempt to stand but eventually I get there. I hold the blanket open for Kyle to see. One side is a navy blue honeycomb print and the other is orange with arrows moving in different directions.

"I like it," he says, as he takes the blanket from me. I reach down and grab the crib shit and take it to the crib and drape it across the side.

"We still don't have a mattress." I facepalm myself and sigh.

"Well, let's go get that taken care of then?" he says, holding his hand out for me. I take it and as we step into the hallway, he shoves me towards my bedroom. "First, go put a shirt on to cover up your boobs. I don't think I can handle anyone else openly checking you out today," I laugh, as I walk over the threshold into my room for a shirt. Seeing Kyle jealous is a huge turn on for me.

When we return from purchasing a mattress and Kyle has it maneuvered into the crib, I work on getting the bedding added and the last few little touches to the room. It's easily my favorite room in the house now.

After Kyle leaves, I take a moment to sit on the couch and watch tv. My feet have been killing me all day. I've had a rough headache all day that I can't seem to shake. I move my feet onto the couch and lay down, adjusting the pillow under my head. Teen Mom is playing reruns on MTV. Very fitting. After a while, I notice I'm beginning to feel worse. I'm nauseous and my vision begins to blur slightly.

I've been sitting for forty minutes without any improvement. I grab my phone. I struggle to call Kyle; my vision goes in and out. I manage to dial his number before my world turns black and I crash against the back of the couch.

# 30

# KYLE

MY PHONE RINGS as I step through my front door. I've just gotten home from Tessa's, I had to stop by the bar on my way and check on a few things. I've been slowly maneuvering myself away from the bar and letting someone else take control so I can focus on Tessa and the baby.

"Hello?" I say, as I press the phone to my ear. I'm expecting to hear her sweet voice on the other end, but I'm greeted with silence. "Tessa?" I pull my phone away from my ear making sure we are still connected.

Silence.

"Tessa? Can you hear me?" Nothing. Not a peep. I can't even hear her breathing. My heart drops as I turn and rush back through my front door. I fumble my keys, I'm so worked up on getting to her. I know something is wrong, I can feel it.

I drop my phone and the screen shatters against the concrete at my feet. When I pick it up the screen is black, and I can't get it to power on.

Shit. Shit. Shit.

I throw open my truck door and jump inside. Not bothering to use my seatbelt, I throw the truck in reverse and fly out of my driveway. My tires squeal as I pull onto the road.

I fly through stop signs and stop lights, blaring my horn each time. It's a shock I'm not getting pulled over, but nothing would stop me from getting to her right now.

When I finally reach her apartment, I barely put my truck in park. I jump out running and leave my truck door wide open. I take the stairs to her apartment three at a time. The door is locked when I get there.

I bang several times, not getting an answer. I finally back away and use my force to kick open the door. Pieces of wood split as it shoves open and I rush through.

Tessa is laying on the couch, completely unconscious.

"Shit." I move to her. "Tessa, baby. Can you hear me?" I gently pat the side of her jaw trying to wake her, but get no movement. My phone is busted up so I search for her phone. It's still in her hand.

I grab it quickly and dial 911.

"911, what's your emergency?" the dispatcher says.

"Help," I shout into the phone.

"Sir, calm down. I need you to tell me your emergency." Calm down?

"She's pregnant and passed out on the couch," I say, trying to keep my voice even so she can understand me.

"Ok. I'm tracing your phone call now. Are you in the home with her?"

"Yes. I'm here." I look back down at Tessa, my heart aches.

"Sir? I'm sending an ambulance to your location. Police are also on their way. Stay on the line with me." I feel relief when I hear that help is coming soon. "Is she breathing at all?" I look at Tessa and watch her chest, but can't see any visible movement.

"I'm not sure. I can't tell."

"Can you find a pulse?" she asks. How the fuck do you check for a pulse?

"Um."

"Either her neck or on her wrist. You will feel it." I choose to try her wrist first. I grab the one closest to me. "You will place two fingers on the inside of her wrist, and you should feel a faint beat." I try, I move my fingers all over trying to press hard enough to feel anything.

"I can't find anything." I continue searching, but come up short, each and every time.

"Try her neck. Her pulse will be right under her jaw, kind of in the crease of her neck. It should be stronger than her wrist." I move my hand to where she says. I press my fingers to the spot and hold still.

I can feel her pulse, it's slow but it's there. A lone tear slips down my cheek and it startles me when if falls to her cheek. I couldn't remember the last time I cried.

"Did you find it?" the dispatcher asks, and I had forgotten I was on the phone.

"Yes, yes. I found it."

"Good. Help is pulling up now, stay with me until they arrive."

Just then, two paramedics come through her front door that is still in pieces from where I kicked it open.

"Please back away, sir." I do as they say, clutching her phone in my hand and watch as they prepare to move her. They lift her from the couch and place her on the gurney before strapping her in tightly. They move her out of the room and I'm hot on their heels. They load her into the back of the ambulance, but don't grant me access to ride, so I run across the parking lot to my truck. Jumping in, I'm putting it in drive before they even have the back doors to the ambulance shut securely.

I follow them closely, staying right with them breaking every law on my way to the hospital. They pull up to the emergency entrance and I park my truck along the curb before jumping out and following them inside.

"Sir?" An older lady places a hand to my chest, stopping me from following through the silver double doors. "Sir," she says louder ,and it catches my attention. I glance down at her and her eyes soften at the sight of me. "Follow me, I have some paperwork for you to fill out while they get her figured out." I don't want to leave this spot. My whole life just rolled through those doors and I am helpless on the other side.

# 31

# KYLE

I'VE BEEN SITTING HERE for what seems like hours, waiting on an update. In the same waiting room I sat in a few weeks ago. I've called my parents and my sister. The nurses keep coming to check on me, but my eyes never leave the emergency room doors they rolled her through.

"Kyle?" My mother's voice floats through the air, offering a tiny bit of comfort. I tear my eyes away from the doors long enough to meet my mother's sad eyes. My father stands behind her, both of their faces are filled with worry. My mother's features soften as she takes in my current state. I'm sure I look like hell after the events of today.

They both take a seat on either side of me, not saying a word. It's exactly what I need right now. My father's strong-arm wraps around my shoulder, squeezing tightly. I rest my elbows on my knees, leaning forward with my head resting in both hands. I can feel the tears soaking the skin of my hands. My mother wraps her arms around my torso and lays her head against my shoulder. I can feel her tears against the sleeve of my shirt.

The double doors open then, and my head snaps up quickly. I see Dr. Kirk and Lou walk through then glance around the waiting area until their eyes land on mine. In a few quick strides, I'm standing in front of them both, waiting for an update.

"Kyle." Lou nods as my parents stand beside me. "As you know, Tessa has preeclampsia." I nod, I remember her discussing this with me before. "Her blood pressure bottomed out again, this time we were unable to stop the labor. The babies were still too small, so we had to move them to the NICU to get them on oxygen."

"How is Tessa?" I ask.

"She's doing well. She should be waking up soon. We had to do an emergency cesarean surgery; it will be a more difficult recovery for her, but completely normal."

I missed the birth of my baby; we didn't get to put forth any of the things we practiced in lamaze class.

Wait. Did she say babies?

"Lou?" I snap my head up to meet her eyes. She's smiling at me. "Did you say babies? As in more than one?"

She nods her head slowly. Her smile growing in size. I hear my parents both gasp with excitement beside me, more tears are falling as my sister takes me in her arms.

"Dr. Kirk has been assigned as their NICU doctor and can give you an update on them," she says, as she turns her attention to Dr. Kirk.

"Yes. The babies are doing really well, while they aren't technically extremely early, they were still underdeveloped and will need this extra little help," he explains. "Would you like to see them?" I move from where I'm standing towards the doors without another word to my parents or my sister. I shove the doors open, waiting for Dr. Kirk to catch up with me.

"Wait." I stop and turn to Dr. Kirk and Lou who just entered the hall behind me. "Did you say babies?" I'm confused why they would refer to my son as babies.

"We did," Dr. Kirk says, with a smile on his face. Lou takes a small step closer to me.

"Somehow we missed the second heartbeat. We had times where we thought we heard a second, but we could never confirm it." I look at my sister, I'm sure my jaw is on the ground after this news. My head is spinning.

"I have twins?" I ask, and my sister nods to confirm. "Does Tessa know?"

"No, the second birth was a surprise to us all," she says. I see my parents through the small window of the door.

He and Lou lead me down a long hall to the elevator. Once Dr. Kirk presses the button to the fourth floor, he explains how well Tessa did in delivery and it makes me smile. I haven't known her for long, but anyone can tell she is strong, especially with her childhood and everything she has gone through. She was unconscious for most of it, but her body responded well.

*Beep. Beep. Beep. Beep.*

That's all you hear as you enter the small room in the nursery. He explained to me that the babies were small, both barely weighing five pounds, but for twins they are a good weight. He explained they had tubing attached to them since they aren't able to eat or breathe on their own still and he wanted to prepare me for the sight.

I step up next to their beds and I'm instantly hit with this longing feeling. I've never felt anything like it before.

They are sharing an incubator and he explains this was the best decision for them as their stats leveled out once they were placed together. He goes on to explain the boy was born two minutes before the girl. They don't have names yet and I need to see Tessa so we can decide.

My daughter is beautiful. She is wrapped in a soft pink blanket and has a small hat over her tiny head. I'm not sure what Tessa looked like as an infant or even a teenager, but I see so many features in our little girl that remind me of her mother already. She has light colored hair that peeks out from under her hat and a cute little nose. Our boy looks more like me, I think. A head full of dark hair. He's wrapped in a baby blue blanket with the same hospital hat on his head. I'm surprised they both have so much hair.

Lou walks into the NICU and steps up beside me. She has changed since I last saw her, replacing her surgery gown for a fresh pair of scrubs. She places her hand in mine and just stands with me staring at my babies.

"They are beautiful, Kyle." She places her hand against the incubator, staring down at her niece and nephew. Her pager beeps several times on her waist. "Tessa is being moved to her own room in recovery, she has just started waking up now. You can see her whenever you'd like." My parents enter the room then, their eyes are automatically drawn to their grandchildren and the smile on my mother's face brightens the room.

I look to my parents, "Stay with them, please." My father nods as my mother wipes her tears and stares down at her grandchildren again. I turn my attention back to Lou, "Take me to her, now." She nods before exiting the room

# 32

# TESSA

I BLINK several times before my eyes fully open and focus. I'm in a hospital bed, machines are beeping around me, a nurse is taking my blood pressure and my stomach feels empty. I glance down and notice the IV in my arm and see the drip of the fluids.

"Where am I?" The nurse places my chart on the bedside table. She moves to check my vitals.

"Hello, Tessa. I'm Veronica, your nurse. You had a spill at home earlier today, I'll go out and find Dr. Tucker so she can explain." Just as the words leave her mouth, Dr. Tucker and Kyle walk through the door. My eyes connect with his and it's obvious he's been crying. My stomach drops thinking the worst has happened to our baby.

"Thank you for paging me, Veronica." Veronica smiles at me, then leaves the room.

"Tessa, how are you feeling?" She grabs my chart and begins flipping through the pages. "Your blood pressure has returned to a normal level now, which is really good after birth."

"I'm fine." I glance between her and Kyle. Kyle's eyes are red and blood shot, his dark hair is a mess. "The baby?" I never take my eyes off Kyle. He smiles softly at me and I'm not sure why, but it calms me. Completely melts my fear away. I know that if something awful would have happened, that he wouldn't be able to smile at me like this. He moves to my bedside and places his hand over mine before he sits off to the side.

Dr. Tucker moves to my other side, looking through the chart the nurse handed her.

"You passed out in your apartment earlier, your blood pressure was extremely high when the paramedics got to the scene. Somehow, you were able to get a call through to Kyle, he rushed to your apartment and found you before calling 911. You were rushed here by ambulance and we were forced to do an emergency c-section. During the c-section, we delivered not one, but two babies, Tessa. A boy and a girl." I gasp and look to Kyle. He's still smiling, his eyes are shining proudly at this news.

"We have two babies. How is this possible? It was never mentioned during the ultrasound appointments." I'm struggling wrapping my mind around the fact that I have two infants. Not one. I'm not at all prepared for this.

"Sometimes they go undetected, not always but in your case, this is what happened."

"What about Tessa? Will she be fine?" Kyle is staring at his sister with a concerned look on his face.

"She will be completely fine. I'll leave you two to talk. Tessa, when you're up to it, I'd like to take you to see your babies." She smiles before leaving the room.

I turn my attention back to Kyle. His handsome face looks exhausted.

"Hi," he says so quietly I almost didn't hear him.

"Hi," I repeat. "Have you been to see them?"

"I have." He smiles at me before grabbing my hand with his. "They are perfect."

"She said a boy and a girl?"

"Yes, the girl looks so much like you and the boy is the spitting image of me. You'll see shortly."

"I'm not prepared for two, Kyle. When do you think I'll be released? I need to get everything ready for them. I'm not ready." I cry into my free hand.

"Hey, hey. It's ok. You don't have to do this on your own, Tessa. I'm here now and I'm not leaving any of you. Whatever you need, I'll get it." He pry's my hands away from my face before he takes them in his own and places soft, sweet kisses to each of my palms. He slowly reaches up, his eyes never leaving mine and gently brushes away the tears.

"We have to talk about all of this eventually, Kyle."

"I know, and we will. We will. Let's just focus on our babies for now. They need names."

## 33

## TESSA

KYLE and I spend the next twenty minutes picking out and discussing names of our babies. He asks if I want to consider my parents for names. I've told him some of the story with my parents before. My mother and I were very close when I was younger, we did everything together when she wasn't working. Anne was her name.

"Kate." He mentions his mother's name is Lucile and explains how Lou was named in a short version of his mother's name. I've never even paid attention to his mother's name, and I feel guilty considering she hosted a baby shower in her home in honor of me.

"Lucy." I pull my attention to his face so I can see the expression.

"Lucy," he repeats. "I like it. I really like it." He kisses my cheek. "Are you sure?"

I nod repeatedly. It seems fitting and I love that they are all here in this hospital and Lou has been so supportive of my entire situation since my first initial visit with her.

"What about her middle name?" I question.

"Hmm. Lucy.. Lucy.." He's thinking extremely hard about this one.

"What do you think about Anne? It was my mother's name."

"Lucy Anne. I like it." He smiles at me and it causes my breath to catch.

"What about my boy?" Kyle scoots back in his seat and crosses his legs. His cocky demeanor makes me laugh and I hope our boy is filled with the confidence of his father.

"What about Layne? That way we could keep the L in both of their names?"

"I like that. I like them having the same first letter. Middle?"

I pause. I'm suddenly nervous and I'm not sure why. "Kyle," I say, as I watch for what I've said to register.

His smile continues to grow. He reaches around me and pulls me gently to him. I lay my head against his chest. A few months ago, I was all alone, prepared to raise a baby all on my own. Now I have this man who says he will go through it all with me, and with two I'll most definitely need the backup.

"Lucy Anne and Layne Kyle. I think they're perfect, Tess. I know we are stuck in this odd predicament, and it's far from how either of us planned our future to turn out, but I just want you to know that whatever you or the babies need I'm here. I'm all in, Tessa. My children will have a father present in their lives. I promise you."

I hug his neck tightly as the tears silently fall. This is not how I expected birth to end up, but it's so much more perfect than I could have imagined it turning out.

## 34

## KYLE

Lou finally gives Tessa permission to go see Lucy and Layne. She's still really sore from the surgery, but we help her into a wheelchair and I'm currently pushing her down the hall towards the elevators now.

"Is it weird that I'm extremely nervous to meet them?" She hasn't quit picking at her thumb nail since we hit the hallway. I lean down and press a kiss to the top of her head.

"Not at all, but baby, everything will be fine." I press the up button on the elevator and wait for it to open on our floor.

"What if they don't remember me? And your parents are still with them, right?" she asks.

"Yes, don't worry they won't leave them alone. You've given them two grandchildren, Tess. Mom and dad are over the moon in love with them. I didn't want them to be alone while I was with you." I maneuver her into the elevator and turn her to face the doors.

"This is so embarrassing, Kyle." She covers her face with her hands, obviously embarrassed. "Having to go everywhere in a gown and having to ask questions about our babies."

"Hey." I grab her hands and slowly pull them away from her beautiful face. One thing I could never forget is how gorgeous her blue eyes are. Those same blue eyes that catch my breath each time I look into them. "Everything is going to be fine. You have nothing to be embarrassed about, I promise." I bring both of her hands to my lips.

*Ding. Ding.*

The elevator doors slide open and we're greeted by my sister.

"Hi Tessa. Still feeling okay?" she asks, concerned. Her eyes bouncing to mine, I'm sure she can see the tear stains on Tessa's cheeks.

"Yes. I'm just anxious." She smiles and my heart skips a beat. I'm not sure what it is, but this woman gave birth to twins this morning and here she is, stitches and all, ready to see her babies.

"Shall we?" My sister holds open the NICU doors for us as I push Tessa through. She leads us to another door where the babies' room is and pushes open the door. Inside are the two incubators, one which has been unplugged and moved aside since both Layne and Lucy prefer to lay together. My parents stand immediately with smiles the size of Texas across their faces.

"Hi Tessa." My mom moves towards us. She bends and kisses Tessa's cheek.

"Hi, pretty girl." My father does the same.

I wheel Tessa closer to the incubator and put her as close as I possibly can to the babies.

"And this, this is Lucy Anne and this is Layne Kyle," I whisper, so only she can hear me. I'm not ready for the rest of the family to hear the names just yet, this needs to be a moment for the two of us and our babies. Out of the corner of my eye, I catch Lou shooing my parents out for us to have a private moment. I silently thank her when her eyes catch mine.

"Hi, Lucy, hi Layne." She stares at them in complete awe of our children. "They are so perfect, Kyle. Absolute perfection."

"They are." I stare at the two of them, they've wiggled closer to each other now.

"How long will they be in the NICU?" Her eyes meet mine, and I catch myself staring deeply into them.

"I'm not sure, let me see if I can find Dr. Kirk and get some more answers." I kiss the top of her head, then exit the room.

Once I return, she's in the same spot as I left her, just staring at our babies so intently. Dr. Kirk enters behind me.

"Tessa, hello. I understand we have figured out names, correct?" He looks between the two of us and I gesture for her to tell him.

"Yes, Lucy Anne and Layne Kyle." We both smile proudly down at them both.

"Beautiful names." He glances behind us at them both. "So, basically, they were born a few weeks early. Their lungs look great but they're having some difficulty breathing on their own, which is why they are connected to this machine and they aren't able to feed on their own, however, Lucy weighed in at four pounds ten ounces and Layne weighed five pounds two ounces. which is a great weight, especially for premature twins." He flips through their chart a few pages. "But, based on their progress so far and their weight I would expect them to be discharged in at least two weeks, unless something changes. Possibly even sooner if they keep progressing." He smiles to Tessa who seems relieved, then shakes my hand.

"Thank you," I tell him, before he exits the room. "What do you think?" Turning my attention back to Tessa.

"I'm relieved they won't be here for too long at least." She places her hand against them, and a tear slides down her cheek.

"Hey, come here." I bend down to her level and pull her to my chest tightly. "Everything is fine, babe. They're both healthy, nothing major is wrong. They'll be home in a few weeks." Tucking a strand of hair behind her ear, I kiss the top of her head. I catch myself doing that more often than not today.

"Yeah? And where is home, Kyle? I have two children by a man I had a one-night stand with. I had to have an emergency c-section that I was unconscious through. I'm only prepared for one baby. I can't hold either of them or feed them. I wanted to breastfeed and now everything is ruined." She sobs into my chest and all I can do is hold her closely. I didn't think about how this would all be affecting her. How much it would gut me to not be able to fix this.

"I'm sorry, Tess. I know this is hard for you, I know. We'll figure all of that out, we will but right now we can only focus on getting them healthy enough to get home to us. You all can move in with me, or I can stay with you to help out. You won't be able to care for them both 24/7 recovering from a c-section and I'm going to be there to help. I'll go out right now and buy everything they need; you just make me a list."

She pushes against me, I release my hold on her, not wanting to, but wanting to give her the space she needs.

"You want to move in together?"

"Why not? I'm their father, you're their mother. This way we can spend all the time we need with them and I can help you."

"Kyle, this is insane. We don't even know each other," she says. "At least, not well enough to move in together."

"Well, then we will get to know each other. What do you say? My place or yours?"

"Kyle, I don't even know where you live. I already have a nursery set up for one baby."

"Fine. It's settled. We will go to your place. It's probably a better choice considering I live above my bar in a two bedroom apartment." I wink at her and she can't help but laugh.

"You told me you didn't live there." She rolls her eyes and I kiss away one of her tears. "This is insane, you realize this right?" She wipes the tears from her cheeks and smiles at me.

"I do." For the first time in eight months, I lean across and kiss the mother of my children, right on the lips and it's just the way I remember it.

# 35

# TESSA

I'm being discharged today. It's already been a week since the twins were born and Lou can't keep me at the hospital any longer. Kyle insists on taking me home while his parents stay with the babies, so I can shower in my own home and get some rest.

I tried to argue, but he wasn't having it.

"You ready to go?" He walks through my hospital door as I'm packing the last bit of my things into my overnight bag.

"I think so." I sit on the edge of the bed as I zip my bag shut. "I just hate being so far away from them."

"I know, but my parents are with them and Lou is on call tonight and will be here most of the night, so they'll be fine. We will get some rest and come back first thing in the morning." I nod in agreement, afraid to speak in fear of crying some more. I'm not really sure how I can even produce anymore tears at this point. All I have done is cry for the past 24 hours since Lou told me she would be discharging me.

"C'mon, baby." He grabs my bag and slings it over his shoulder and holds out his other hand for me. I love when he calls me baby, even though we aren't in a relationship, it's really nice to be cared for by someone else. I remember him being similar during our night together, very catering.

I'm silent on the way home. Thinking about the twins and how they should be in the backseat right now with us.

We pull into my driveway and I notice my front door is a different color. "What?" I look at Kyle for an explanation.

"Yeah, I kind of kicked it in when you passed out and I couldn't get ahold of you." He has no guilt on his face when he says it, and I'm truly thankful that he rushed over when he did.

Once we park, Kyle is quick to grab my bag and open the door for me. He has to help me in and out because it's so tall and my stitches still pull like a bitch.

We walk hand in hand to the front door, he pulls my keys from his back pocket and unlocks the door pushing it open for me to walk through.

Once inside, I look around and realize there are boxes everywhere. A new car seat, a double stroller, tons of shopping bags, everything we could possibly need for twins.

"Where did all of this come from?" I walk to the pile and start going through the bags. Little blue and pink onesies, bath towels, bottles. Everything we got at the shower, now also in the color pink.

"Some came from mom and dad, some from Lou and some from Chloe, but most of it I picked up the other day when I installed your new door. I didn't want you to stress about anything that wasn't done." I stand and walk to him, press up on my toes and kiss him across the lips. It's the first time I've made the move and he smiles when we break apart.

"Thank you." It's all I can think to say. This relieved so much of the stress I have been feeling.

He smiles down at me and tucks my hair behind my ear. "Now. You need to shower. What do you want to eat and I'll order some food?"

"Chinese sounds good. It's been a while and it's my favorite."

We spend the rest of the night sitting on my living room floor, surrounded in baby gear discussing how perfect the twins are.

"At some point, we need to determine what we plan to do here." I sit my box of noodles on the coffee table and slowly adjust myself so I'm facing him. I move at snail speed and can't seem to move any quicker, regardless of how hard I try.

"I agree, but either way I want to be with my kids as much as possible. I never saw myself with a family, certainly not in the way this all played out, but I'm glad it happened." He places his box beside mine. "I don't know what this is between us, but I do think it could be more."

My breathing picks up, and I'm suddenly nervous. That was the last thing I expected him to say. My feelings for him continue to grow the more time I spend with him and watch him with our twins.

"Do you want it to be more?" My hair has fallen across my face and as always, Kyle gently tucks it behind my ear before placing a soft kiss just below my ear. Chill bumps break out across my skin.

"I do." He leans in and places his lips against mine. Soft but sure. It is single-handedly the best kiss of my life.

# 36

## TESSA

I WAKE up the next morning feeling completely rested. Dr. Tucker gave me some medicine that would help me rest and it certainly worked. I can't figure out if I should call her Lou or keep with the formal, I didn't expect my OB to end up being the father of my unborn child's sister.

*This is the type of luck I have. I swear.*

I've barely slept between the uncomfortable hospital bed, the tug of the stitches across my abdomen and running back and forth to spend as much time as possible with the twins. I've worn myself down and as much as I hate to admit, I needed this rest.

I roll over expecting to find Kyle beside me in bed, but he is nowhere to be found. I'm not sure if I'm disappointed or relieved. I don't have the best bed head or morning breath.

The smell of bacon makes its way to my nostrils and I'm quickly and painfully climbing out of bed in search of clean clothes. I dress quickly and brush my teeth at light-ning speed, hospital food has not been appealing and the

Chinese from last night just wasn't enough after a full week of frozen chicken nuggets.

Once I step into the kitchen area, I notice Kyle immediately. He's only wearing his jeans, that are hung low on his hips, his black boxers peak out over the top of his jean line. He's shirtless with several tattoos covering his torso and arms. It's ridiculous how attracted I am to this man and his sculpted back. One tattoo is free and as I step closer, I notice they are two small footprints with our children's names written above them. My heart swells at the sight of it.

As if sensing my presence, Kyle turns, capturing my eyes easily. His gaze slowly slides down my body and that perfect smirk appears. God he is so damn sexy.

"Good morning." Kyle turns his attention back to flipping pancakes on the stove. "Hungry? I made pancakes."

I inhale deeply, causing my stomach to growl. Kyle laughs as I slowly slide onto one of the bar stools. "God, yes!" He slides a plate in front of me then passes me the syrup. "Thank you."

He rounds the island and slides into a seat next to me as I take a bite, then a second.

"Whoa, babe. Easy," he laughs, as he leans in to kiss my temple.

"I'm starving. And that hospital food was awful."

"I would have run and got you something different." He drops his fork to look at me.

"I know, I was just more focused on hurrying to eat so I could go help with the twins." I sigh, taking another bite. "They were my top priority."

"I'm proud of you," he says. It catches me off guard and

some of the orange juice dribbles down my chin. "You've been amazing through this entire process."

Words escape me, so all I can manage is a smile in return.

Just as we're finishing up, and Kyle is loading the dishwasher my phone rings from the bedroom.

As fast as I possibly can, I run to the bedroom for my phone.

"Hello," I sound breathless, trying to get the word out once I realize it's the hospital.

"Tessa, hi. This is Dr. Kirk. I have some good news." He pauses. "Both Layne and Lucy are breathing on their own and have been removed from the ventilators for nearly three hours. If all continues to go as planned, we will remove their feeding tubes shortly and you and Mr. Tucker may come feed them their first bottles."

"Oh my gosh. That is wonderful news." Silent tears begin to fall. "Thank you so much, Dr. Kirk."

"You're very welcome. I'll see you both shortly."

The call disconnects and I'm sobbing uncontrollably at this point. Kyle walks through the door and immediately becomes panicked.

"Tess. What's wrong?" He slowly wipes the tears that continue to fall. "Babe?"

"The twins." I bring my eyes to his. "They're breathing on their own and we.." I pause once I see the look in his eyes. They're so full of love for his children, this man who loves them both so much already and two months ago didn't even know he would become a father so soon.

"Baby?"

"We can go to the hospital shortly to feed them their first bottles."

I wait. Kyle slowly begins to smile one of the most breathtaking smiles I have witnessed yet.

"That's great." He has me wrapped in his arms immediately. "Let's get ready to go."

Once we're both changed, we make quick work of grabbing anything needed for the twins and head to Kyle's truck.

"We should probably get the car seats installed soon." I twist glancing into the backseat. "At least you have more space than I do."

Kyle quickly glances to the back, then back at the road. "Yeah, I'll get everything situated tonight and install the extra car seat bases in your car."

The rest of the ride is quiet, both of us swimming in our thoughts. How are the twins today? Are they alone? Are his parents still there? What about Lou? So many thoughts cross my mind in that fifteen-minute car ride. I'm anxious to see my babies and finally get to touch them. That's probably been the hardest part of all, staring through a glass box. Not smelling their baby breath or feeling their soft skin.

We pull into the hospital parking lot; Kyle offers to drop me at the door, but I decline. I, both, want to walk in with him but I also feel as though I *need* him for this.

Once we reach the NICU floor, his parents step out of the double doors.

"Hi Mom." Kyle bends to hug his mother, the smile on her face is infectious. "Dad." He shakes his father's hand, then returns his hand to mine. His parents follow the movement with their eyes and I don't miss the way his mom nudges his dad with her elbow.

"The babies are waiting for you both. Go." His mother

166 | ONE NIGHT

shoos us to the entrance. "We will be in the waiting room if you need us." She smiles at me and I'm grateful they're here for the twins.

The room is quiet compared to the last time I entered. The machine screens are black and my heart screams with joy. They have both been removed from the previous incubator and placed into a large hospital crib.

"Hello." Dr. Kirk greets us as we step near their crib. "We attempted to separate them into bassinets but these two are stubborn," he chuckles, and places his clipboard on a nearby table. "These two will be inseparable, I have no doubt." Dr. Kirk takes his stethoscope from around his neck, placing the bell against Laynes little chest. He slowly moves it from spot to spot, then places it against Lucy. Kyle and I stand quietly watching, he hasn't removed his hand from the small of my back. "Everything sounds good, we're a go for their first bottle feeding."

On cue, a nurse walks in with two small bottles of premixed infant formula, two small nipples and two burp rags.

"Have a seat." She ushers us into two rocking chairs that have been placed near the far wall. Kyle and I each take a seat, eager. "We will send you home with several packages of these, they seem to do well with this formula." She shakes the small bottles for a few moments, then places the nipple on the top. She hands each of us a bottle and a burp rag, Kyle holds it up then mouths to me *what is this for?*. I laugh silently. Parenthood will be a walk in the park for him, obviously.

She brings Layne to me, easily placing him in my arms. He's so tiny but I can tell he will be built similar to his father. His dark hair is brushed to the side and he smells like Johnson's pink baby lotion. I bring him close to my face, just breathing in his sweet baby smell.

"Are you sniffing him?" Kyle asks. His face is comical, he really has no idea how sweet the smell is.

"Just you wait." Just then the nurse places Lucy in his arms. He's stiff for a moment, then slowly begins to relax. "You won't hurt her, she's fine." He smiles at me halfheart-edly, he's nervous and it is single handedly the cutest thing I have ever seen.

He begins relaxing and brings his nose close to Lucy and inhales. I laugh, loud enough that Layne startles in my arms.

"Ok, I get it. They do smell pretty good, huh?" the nurse laughs, then gives Kyle some assistance so he can get comfortable.

"Sometimes they are difficult to wake, you'll learn what works and what doesn't work. My children always had to be stripped to a diaper and a cool rag or cool hands touching them before they'd wake up and realize they could eat." She turns and begins writing in their charts. "They can each drink up to 2 ounces, if they can handle it. I recom-mend burping every little bit to keep gas away. I'll let you all have some privacy." She smiles before exiting the room.

"What do you think, daddy?" I ask Kyle. He's been staring down at his little girl, completely entranced by her.

"She's perfect." His eyes collide with mine and I could melt from the intensity of his stare. "What about you, momma?"

I look from Lucy to Layne and sigh. I'm so content in this moment. My babies are both healthy and beating all the odds for twins.

"They're perfect." I kiss Layne's temple.

# 37

# TESSA

WE'VE BEEN TRYING to settle into a routine since we came home from the hospital. The babies are three months old already and time seems to be flying so quickly.

Lucy and Layne are growing right on track and have my entire heart, except when they are wide awake at three am and refuse to go back to sleep.

Kyle has stayed here since we brought the babies home from the hospital. At first, he slept on the couch, but I know that couch isn't comfortable for everyday use so I forced him to move to my room with me.

Our relationship is complicated, having two infants and not knowing if you are technically in a relationship or not is hard. He kisses me good morning when I wake up and goodnight before I fall asleep, but I'm still unsure where his mind is in everything and really need to discuss this with him.

Lou has been begging to keep the babies for us so we can get some free time, so tonight I've decided I will take her up on the offer. It's a Monday night, which is an odd "date night" if that's what you want to call it, but with Kyle running a bar, our nights aren't the same as others.

I'm running around like a crazy person when Kyle walks through the door, the babies are in their swings that are placed in front of the large picture window we have in the living room. It's one of their favorite places.

"What's going on?" he asks, as he walks over to where the twins are and places a soft kiss on both of their heads. It's something he does every day when he gets home, and it's one of my favorite moments to watch between them.

"Your sister is watching the babies tonight and I'm trying to make sure they have everything they need." I grab their car seats and sit them on the dining room table. I look around the room and try to run through a mental list of things the babies will need. I've pumped enough milk over the last three months that we have a freezer full and will more than likely have to purchase a deep freeze at this rate. "I think that's everything." I turn to look at him, really look at him now.

He's wearing my favorite jeans, they are dark wash with just a little wear to them, but they fit him so good. He's wearing a t-shirt, but it completes his look, making him sexy as hell. His eyes are roaming my body just as mine were doing to his.

I haven't dressed up since probably my baby shower, I hardly have any clothes that fit since I'm still not back down to pre-pregnancy weight and all the maternity clothes are now far too big. I did however manage to slip into a pair of jeans, that's an accomplishment on its own. They are a little too tight but I'm desperate tonight. My shirt is just a tank top with a cardigan layered over the top, nothing special.

"You look gorgeous," he says, as he steps up beside me and places a kiss on my temple. I blush and turn to grab one of the twins to buckle them in their car seat. This is still my least favorite part of being a parent, I'm always afraid I'm going to pinch one of their little fingers in the chest clip.

Lucy is my easy child, but Layne, well he will fight you to the ends of the Earth when it comes to his car seat. He hates it.

"So, where are we going?" Kyle asks, as he places Layne in his car seat and begins to buckle him. I won't admit it, but I'm kind of glad he has to fight with Layne for a minute and it'll give me a break with the car seat.

"Just out to eat, nowhere fancy. I don't want to be away from them for too long," I say. I haven't left their sides since they've been born, other than taking naps while either Kyle's parents or Kyle was in the living room with them.

The drop off at Lou's goes smoothly, Kyle's parents end up being there. Lou's boyfriend, Peter, was leaving as we arrived. He barely acknowledged us in passing. Kyle says he's always been a douche and can't figure out what Lou sees in him.

We decide to do a quick little burger joint downtown called, Marvelous. It's supposed to be one of the best, but I haven't had the chance to eat here yet. The waitress comes to take our drink order and of course openly flirts with Kyle in front of me, I roll my eyes and try not to let it bother me. He just has such a sexy face it's hard for girls, I get it.

"So,-" I say, as I place my menu on the table and lean forward on my elbows. "I wanted to talk to you tonight."

"Oh?" He takes a quick sip of his drink and I'm caught staring at his Adam's apple as he swallows. "What about?"

"Us," I say. I'm nervous for this conversation, but I know it needs to happen.

"What about us?"

"What are we? I mean, you stay at my house every night, you come straight there after work aside from running home and changing." I pick at my thumb nail. "I just don't know what is really going on between us."

"I thought it was obvious?" he says. I look up to be met with his dark blue eyes, I could easily get lost in them. "I want to be with you, Tess. Like all the way. I'm sick of going to my place to get clothes, I want all of my things mixed in with yours. I want it to feel like it's home, that way the babies have both of their parents all the time." He sighs before taking my hands in his. "I want us. I want a future with you." My lips slowly spread to a smile at his words and I am suddenly no longer hungry.

"Take me home," I say. Before I have a chance to reach for my purse, Kyle is already throwing money down on the table to pay for our drinks that will go wasted. He grabs my hand and pulls me behind him out of the restaurant.

When we get to my apartment, Kyle shoves the key I gave him into the door and turns it slowly, allowing me to enter first. The lights are off but there is a soft glow of lights, just like in his bar that are stretched across my living room. There is a bottle of wine on the bar with two glasses sitting filled beside it.

"What is all this?" I ask, as I turn to look at Kyle's face, he has to be just as shocked as me. When I turn, he isn't behind me any longer. It takes me a moment to realize that he is squatted to the ground. When my eyes take him in, I gasp. My hand flying to my mouth to cover the squeal.

"What are you doing?" I ask, as a tear slowly starts to fall.

"Tessa, you were unexpected. I never thought that when you walked into my bar that night, exactly one year ago today, that I'd have found my forever. I didn't realize what I wanted in life until I found you and our babies. It may have all been unconventional, but baby I love how our story was written and I cannot wait to write the rest with you by my side. I want to grow old with you, and watch our children grow together. I love you, Tessa. Will you marry me?"

Our lives were changed one year ago tonight; I hadn't realized the date, but I'm so impressed that he remembered. Tonight, I planned to ask him what the future held for us, but he beat me to the punch. I look down at the man kneeling before me, he's my forever.

"Yes," I say, before I tackle him to the ground.

The End

# THANK YOU

Thank you for taking the time to read One Night, my very first book.

Never miss a new release:
    https://bit.ly/2N2R27V

Join J. Akridge's ARC team:
    https://bit.ly/3gF7uXb

More about J. Akridge's books:
    https://www.jakridgeauthor.com

**Want more?**
    Lou's story is coming soon! PreOrder today!
    Turn the page to get a sneak!

Lou's book is full of heartache, steam, and a happily ever after that will make you SWOON!

Keep scrolling for the preorder!

Want to know the best part? You get a glimpse of Kyle and Tessa, and of course the twins!

# ONE MORE NIGHT

PROLOGUE: Lou

### Fifteen Years Earlier

"WHY ARE YOU DOING THIS? What did I do wrong?" I ask, the tears burning the back of my eyelids. I feel my heart shattering in my chest, and I hate it. I don't know how to fix it, or how to get him to listen to me.

It wasn't supposed to be this way. We were supposed to get married, have children, and live a long life together. It's what we always planned.

Why is he doing this? To me? To us? To our future?

Declan is my best friend and my soulmate. I know I won't ever get over this type of heartache if he walks away.

He turns, walking away from me. I reach out, grabbing his elbow and spin him to face me. His brown hair falls to his forehead as he settles, he looks everywhere but at me.

"Talk to me," I demand. "It's the least you could do." For a moment, I see his wall start to collapse. His eyes soften as he looks at me, I just need to understand why he's doing this to us. "Is this about your dad?" And just like that, that simple question causes that wall to slide back into place. A stone mask covering his face now, not letting me in. "Just talk to me, we can work this out. Please!" I beg.

"It has to be this way, Lou." His green eyes bounce between mine. The look he gives me exposes my biggest fear. He's leaving, he's done, and there's nothing I can do or say right now that's going to change that. "Go home," he mutters before he turns and walks away again.

This time I don't stop him, I watch as he disappears. My feet are rooted to the ground beneath me, and I'm unable to move. So many emotions are flooding me right now, but at the same time... I feel numb.

He reaches his truck, hand frozen on the handle as his head falls forward against the window before he climbs into it. I watch and wait, knowing he's going to climb out and come back to me. He'll tell me it's all a mistake and that he's just struggling with the death of his father. It's only been two weeks, that's normal to still feel emotions like this, right? I've never lost anyone in my life, so I'm not sure what that feels like.

Maybe I wasn't there enough for him. If he needed some time to himself, I could have given him that. I would do anything for him, doesn't he know that?

His head never turns in my direction as he backs out of his parking spot and drives in the opposite direction of his house. We live in a small town, where everyone knows everyone and there's only one place that road leads... and it's far away from here.

Realization sets in that he isn't coming back. He broke up with me. He left me here and broke my heart.

I collapse to the ground beneath me, feeling the weight of my broken relationship on top of me. I don't fight the tears as they fall, my entire world just drove away without an explanation.

I'll never get over Declan Sanchez.

Ever.

# ACKNOWLEDGMENTS

*To my amazing husband*, *my biggest supporter*. Without you, I wouldn't be able to write the way I do. You're always offering a listening ear, even when you don't want to hear about the "smut". Thank you for being you and my rock in this life.

*The indie community*. Whew. THANK YOU! The support from readers, authors, bloggers, bookstagrammers, TikTokers, etc. You're amazing and I'm so thankful to be part of it.

*Of course, thank you to my sweet friend, Nicole*. She helped make this book the very best that it could be.

*Amanda Walker*, you once again killed the cover for me. Thank you so much for taking my ramblings and making them beautiful, because we all know I have no clue what I really want.

*To all the bloggers ... I know you're there.*

Thank you so much for always supporting me and taking on these new books.

*To all of my beta readers,* thank you for always taking the time to work on my books and find any and everything that can make it that much better for the readers. You do so much for me and I love you all for it.

*And finally, thank you to my readers.* Without you, none of this world would be happening. You all keep me motivated more than you know. With every comment, like, share, etc. I see it and I push to give you more. Thank you all for your support and allowing me to continue this dream of writing.

With Love,

# ALSO BY J. AKRIDGE

*The Hawks Series*

Full Court Press

Foul Shot

Bank Shot

Break Away

Blocked Shot

Come Back

*Stand Alone Titles*

One Night

One More Night

Charged: A Salvation Society Novel

Slade

*The Tribute Series*

Enthralled

Enamoured

Enraptured

45597956R00107